Shades of Rome

Ghostly Tales of Roman Britain

F. K. Young

ST JURMIN
PRESS

© Francis Young 2023

Francis Young has asserted his moral right under the Copyright, Designs and Patents Act, 1988, to be identified as the author of this book.

First published 2023
St Jurmin Press
Peterborough, United Kingdom

A catalogue record for this book is available from the British Library

ISBN 978-1-4709-6020-9

These stories are works of fiction. Names, characters, events and incidents are the products of the author's imagination. Any resemblance to actual persons, living or dead, or actual events is purely coincidental.

For Ruth and Anna-Rose

Contents

Preface: Britain's Roman Uncanny	v
Saturnalia	1
To The Unclean Spirits	17
The Green Girl	32
Defixio	49
Abcester	67
Nighthawk	87
The Shrubton Oracle	100

Preface

Britain's Roman Uncanny

In her 2013 book about the cultural impact of Roman Britain, *Under Another Sky*, Charlotte Higgins observed that "'Roman Britain' has become an imaginative space in which some of our darkest anxieties and fantasies have been rehearsed." This is no less true of supernatural fiction than it is of Britain's collective cultural imaginings of Roman violence and colonial subjugation. Beginning with Arthur Machen (1863–1947), who was inspired by his upbringing in the midst of the Roman ruins of Caerleon, the Roman past has been a recurring theme of British supernatural and weird fiction. From John Buchan's novel *Witch Wood* (1927) to Machen's notorious novella *The Great God Pan* (1894) and Algernon Blackwood's unsettling short story 'Roman Remains' (1948), Britain's Roman past inspired dark tales of recrudescent pagan powers threatening the modern world.

Late nineteenth- and early twentieth-century British fascination with Roman Britain may have owed something to the development of scientific archaeology and the wealth of discoveries being made at the time, but the fact that Roman Britain held up a mirror to imperial Britain was no doubt also significant. While the British Empire was avowedly engaged in a 'civilising' mission to bring British law and Christianity to the world, less than two thousand years earlier Britain had itself been a province of an empire with an ostensibly very different set of values. Victorian and Edwardian Britons were simultaneously repelled and intrigued by the sheer *otherness* of pagan Roman Britain. And, crucially, while prehistory and the so-called 'Dark Ages' were perennially captivating, Roman Britain was part of a world studied by every English public schoolboy, who learnt its language and knew the names of its gods.

While the Romans may not have left anything in Britain quite as monumental or iconic as Stonehenge, it is only in recent centuries that Britain's Roman past came to be largely hidden from public view. Probably writing some time in the sixth century – an era of British warlords and Germanic conquest in the wreckage of the former Roman province – Gildas alluded to the still visible images of the gods of Roman Britain: "… the truly diabolical monstrosities of my native country, almost surpassing those of Egypt in number, of which we behold some, of ugly features, to this day within or without their deserted walls, stiff with fierce visage as was the custom." However, even if the visitor to most British cities does not casually run into the sort of remains that still stand in Italy or the south of France, the fact that Roman archaeology yields evidence from a literate culture means that our knowledge of Roman and Romano-British beliefs far exceeds what we know of any other past pagan culture in the island of Britain. Admittedly, this is still not a great deal; archaeology piles name upon name of deities of whom we know almost nothing. We do not know the stories people told about their gods and spirits, and we do not really know (except in general terms) how they were worshipped. Debate still rages among scholars about the extent to which Roman Britain was a thinly Romanised native culture or a heavily

Romanised culture that had to re-invent 'native-sounding' deities.

Yet for all our knowledge of Roman Britain and its strange world of belief, comparatively few writers of supernatural and weird fiction have drawn inspiration from Roman Britain. One reason for this is perhaps because Roman Britain is a world apart from our own, as the title of Higgins's book *Under Another Sky* itself suggests. A dark sundering sea lies between us and antiquity, in a way that it does not between us and the people of the Middle Ages, who inhabited a prototype of our own culture. Thus it was that, for M. R. James, the uncanny past that breaks into the prosaic present was most often medieval, or later – but most certainly not *Roman*. The people of Roman Britain inhabited a different country, spoke a different language, knew different place-names – at least from an English perspective; and in this respect it is perhaps noteworthy that the most determined proponent of the Romano-British weird was a Welshman, Machen. English and Welsh perceptions of continuity and discontinuity with the Roman past are very different. At the same time, however, even the preference of the Celtic nations, over the last two centuries, has been for tales of Britain's 'Celtic twilight': the period *after* the Romans abandoned Britain.

If the *ancientness* of Roman Britain is one reason why the Romano-British uncanny has attracted little attention, its *recentness* may be another. The rise of scientific anthropology in the early twentieth century fuelled tremendous interest in the prehistoric, and contributed to a genre of 'archaeological weird tale' in which survivals of prehistoric rites (often associated with prehistoric landscape features) intrude into the present. The sheer depth of our ignorance of prehistory allowed twentieth-century writers to project contemporary anthropological theories honed on living peoples in Africa and the Pacific onto imagined prehistoric inhabitants of Britain. The prevailing obsession with 'ancient survivals' in folklore and customs that has come to be most associated with Margaret Murray was focussed, for whatever reason, on survivals from the Neolithic. The Romans had very little role to play, except perhaps as supposed suppressors and oppressors of an alleged ancient Neolithic fertility religion, like the Christians who followed them.

For a variety of cultural reasons, then, the 'Roman weird' has been somewhat culturally marginal within British culture and supernatural writing, even if Roman ghosts have sometimes captured the popular imagination – most notably the legionaries seen by Harry Martindale marching through the cellar of the Treasurer's House in York in 1953. A notable exception to the absence of *Romanitas* in British weird writing is, perhaps, the late Victorian and early twentieth-century obsession with the god Pan, who seems to have been so attractive precisely because he represented the antithesis of Victorian social mores. However, since there is vanishingly little evidence for the worship of Pan in Roman Britain, those stories that do imagine a Pan-cult in Britain (such as Machen's *Great God Pan* and H. D. Everitt's 'The Next Heir' (1920)) are a little fanciful. Stories inspired by the archaeology of Roman Britain itself are a little thin on the ground, and it is this niche that the present collection seeks to fill.

*

Just as M. R. James and many other historians after him have made use of the antiquarian ghost story as an outlet for the phenomenology of grappling with the past, so these stories emerged from my own study of Roman Britain's world of belief for my nonfiction writing. The strangeness of that Roman world of belief is a recurring theme of the stories, as is the unsettling co-existence of Roman sacred sites alongside a modern Britain both divorced from their meaning and often unaware of them. While these stories are perhaps better described as 'weird tales' than as 'ghost stories' (there are, after all, few traditional ghosts in them), they deal with a variety of unwelcome intrusions of the Roman past into the present. In 'Saturnalia' an inadvertent offering to a water spirit wakes something unpleasant from the Roman past, while in 'To The Unclean Spirits' the action is triggered by archaeology students hunting for an unusual altar best left in the past. The theme of 'The Green Girl' is the interaction of medieval people with the Roman past, and its echoes down to the present day in a Suffolk village. In *Defixio*, an Oxford academic narrowly escapes disaster after reading an ancient curse tablet, while 'Abcester' explores the consequences of de-consecrating a church that contains Roman religious artefacts. 'Nighthawk' turns to the world of illegal excavation of Roman antiquities; a criminal metal detectorist who is forced to destroy a beautiful Roman artefact suffers the consequences. The final story in the collection, 'The Shrubton Oracle', imagines the potential consequences of a full-scale reconstruction of a Roman temple once renowned for its oracle of Apollo.

    I am grateful to Helen Grant for permission to include the story 'To The Unclean Spirits', which originally appeared in the magazine *Ghosts & Scholars* (no. 43) in November 2022.

Serpentine Green, Peterborough
January 2023

Saturnalia

David felt immense relief when Jonathan Gresveney offered him and Jessica the chance to spend Christmas at Pucklemere. At last, the couple could escape the drama of both their divorces and spend some time together, and Jonathan was hardly burdensome company in a building as large as Pucklemere Hall. He and David had known one another since their undergraduate days, but Jonathan was one of those people nothing ever happens to, and thus they stay forever the same. Jonathan, at forty, was still the same witty aesthete he had been at eighteen; the recipient of inherited wealth that made the thought of serious work laughable, he seemingly showed no interest in relationships with either sex, while being gifted with ageless good looks. And yet, somehow, Jonathan was not rendered insufferable by privilege; David had received proofs enough over the decades that Jonathan's generosity was genuine, and his attachment to the ties of friendship deep.

"You absolutely must both come and stay with me at Pucklemere while it blows over; I'll be as quiet as a mouse, you'll barely see me, I promise," Jonathan assured David over the phone. "Of course, the place is so damn big you'll be lucky to find me anyway."

Jonathan was right about the size of Pucklemere. His parents had lived there until age and infirmity led them to relocate to the family's Mayfair flat, and now Jonathan spent part of the year at Pucklemere when he wasn't wandering aimlessly around Europe, 'absorbing culture'. It was a medieval site; moated, but with a hotchpotch of Georgian additions that were apparently part of a grand scheme of rebuilding – mercifully never fully executed by Jonathan's Gresveney ancestors, leaving behind a palimpsest of a house that David loved. He remembered his first visit to Pucklemere as clearly as if it had been yesterday – the breathless excitement as he crossed the moat into the courtyard, embraced by the arms of the house; the furious rush to see every room he could with his other student friends, suddenly liberated to explore this unimaginable palace; and the air of mystery that surrounded those parts of the house they couldn't access …

He had been back many times since then, of course, and the house had lost much of its mystery – but none of its charm. Perhaps it was the absolute flatness of West Norfolk, and the house's total isolation, that rendered it all the cosier as a place to stay in winter – like lodging in a warm lighthouse in the midst of a raging sea, or something. But the very thought of Pucklemere, for David, conjured the smell of woodsmoke and spiced wine, or the soothing sight of candlelight playing on old tapestries. He had spent Christmas there once before, in his twenties, and Pucklemere quickly became a dreamtime of lost youth he longed to return to, even if the presence of his now ex-wife on that occasion soured the memory a little. But the privilege of introducing Jessica to the place, as if everything were new once again – that was what he yearned for, as much as for Jessica herself.

The couple agreed to meet at Watlington Station. They spent a few blissful minutes on the platform, oblivious of anyone else, before Jonathan rolled up in a battered, mud-bespattered and ancient Land Rover for the drive to

Pucklemere. As always, he was immaculately dressed in a double-breasted black velveteen coat and a yellow silk scarf, the roguish wave of his hair showing no sign of receding in his fifth decade.

"Don't let me interrupt you two lovebirds," he declared, "Imagine I'm not even here."

"Don't be ridiculous, Jon!" David declared, as he embraced Jonathan warmly. "I'm here to see you too, you know I am."

"And this must be the lovely Jessica I've heard so much about …" Jonathan bowed comically to David's lover. For a split-second David sensed his friend inspecting her intensely, as if evaluating whether her charms justified David's divorce from Marina. Or perhaps it was just that a man like Jonathan, for whom relationships apparently meant so little, struggled to comprehend a decision as momentous and financially ruinous as David's in leaving his wife.

"It's lovely to meet you." He took her hand in his, and they climbed into the car.

"I simply can't believe I'm going to be having another Christmas at Pucklemere!" David exclaimed above the sound of the engine, "Do you remember our peacock banquet all those years ago?"

"Christmas? More like Saturnalia, old boy. Don't forget our Roman dining room! I fear there won't be any peacock this time, but I can certainly rustle up the odd pheasant."

Pucklemere's Roman dining room was the one part of the Georgian extension Jonathan's ancestors had actually completed, stretching south onto the old Elizabethan bowling green. On his return from the Grand Tour, the ill-fated Sir Basset Gresveney, who drowned in the mere, commissioned a new summer dining room modelled on the newly discovered rooms he had seen at Pompeii. He had it decorated with mock-Roman frescoes and some genuine bronze and marble statues he brought back from Italy, along with a real Roman mosaic of the Hydra, exquisite in its workmanship, above the fireplace. The most extraordinary part of the story was that, in laying the foundations for the extension, Sir Basset's workmen had come across the bases of ancient walls that the antiquary William Cole confidently identified as Roman; so that it turned out Sir Basset's pastiche sat on top of what was, presumably, a real Roman villa.

David – whose degree in Classics seemed a long time ago but still occasionally came in handy in the Civil Service – remembered an engraving in one of the corridors that depicted the excavations. It suggested fragments of plaster still clinging to the stonework, and showed the serried ranks of brick *pilae* that made a hypocaust – a tell-tale sign of a bathhouse, a villa, or some sort of high-status building. At the risk of occasional mockery from Jonathan, David had spent hours gazing at Pucklemere's medieval walls trying to pick out reused Roman bricks and tiles – for if there was a Roman building under it, the medieval builders of Pucklemere had surely salvaged something from a ruin that could have been standing above ground back then. But David's results were inconclusive – there were a few bricks and tiles he thought might be Roman, but he could hardly prove it. Pucklemere would have to make do with Sir Basset's Georgian pastiche and his rather miscellaneous collection of ancient objets d'art for its *Romanitas*, while its Roman secrets remained long since buried over, and perhaps deliberately destroyed.

The thought planted by Jonathan – that this wasn't to be Christmas, with all its painful associations of family, conflict and craven compromise – but rather *Saturnalia*, comforted David. Saturnalia, the festival of misrule: that he could live with. The duties of Christmas, not so much. It was a joy for him and Jessica to be together, to be sure; but Jessica's discomfort at being away from her daughter Chloe, and David's guilt about his sons, were dark clouds over their delight. In truth, 'Christmas' was not a word either of them wanted to hear.

The light was already fading as the Land Rover pulled off the road and onto a long, bumpy drive that led towards tall, rook-infested beeches. Behind these lay Pucklemere, hidden from view until the very last delicious moment. On the left, another clump of trees marked out the ancient mere that gave the place its name. The rest was a mud-scuffed parkland, scattered with bedraggled-looking sheep and a few trees – some of them felled in last year's storm, and now growing moss on their bleached roots, turned unnaturally towards heaven. With the easy air of a proprietor, Jonathan parked the car haphazardly in the courtyard and ushered David and Jessica within.

*

Jonathan had assured the couple that the main kitchen was theirs, but on the first night of their stay he insisted on treating them to a meal he cooked himself – a treat indeed, since Jonathan was a subtle and discerning cook, and had even once dallied with training as a chef at a Michelin-starred restaurant somewhere; David forgot where, but then Jonathan had dallied with so many things. They did not dine grandly – simply at the big pine table in the kitchen – but Jessica seemed in awe of her surroundings, and the way in which money did not seem to matter to Jonathan. When he emerged from his cellar with a cobweb-covered bottle of wine she even asked him how much it might sell for. On hearing the answer, she was incredulous for a long time that Jonathan planned to open it.

"But my dears, we're celebrating!" He pulled out the ancient cork and began to decant the vintage claret, which glowed ruby red as it splashed to its cut-glass destination.

"To love! To life!" Jonathan toasted, once they all had glasses in their hands. "Io Saturnalia!"

David willingly re-echoed the words, although he was not entirely sure Jessica knew what Saturnalia was.

*

The next morning was a beautiful, bright December day of just the kind David had hoped for. It was perfect for showing Jessica the outside of the house, the mere, and the park. Jonathan, true to his word, was nowhere to be seen; so the couple took a leisurely stroll around the edge of the moat, as David pointed out a few features of the house – even if he was more interested in Jessica's reactions, and her smile, than in anything he could remember about quoins or oriels. In due course he proposed a walk to the mere. They held hands as they picked their way along the rocky path, Jessica in a rather outsized pair of borrowed Wellington boots from Jonathan.

"The mere's some sort of glacial feature, I think," David observed as the dark water came into view. "Left behind when the Ice Age ended and the glaciers all melted. The house is named after it – Pucklemere."

"What does the 'Puckle' bit mean, then?" asked Jessica.

"I think it's an Anglo-Saxon word for a little spirit, or something." They were standing by the water now. "I suppose they must have worshipped the mere; thought something lived in it. The Romans did too. A few years back

Jonathan's dad dredged a whole load of Roman lead piping out of it, like it was some sort of ornamental water shrine or something. And a few of those folded bits of lead, the curse tablet things. It's hard to believe now, isn't it?"

The mere, if it had ever been mastered by the Romans, had long since returned to nature. Jessica smiled. "I love it that you know so much about history," she said, as she pulled David towards her for a long and passionate kiss. At last she broke it. Her right hand fingered her left nervously, and she looked up into her lover's eyes.

"I want to be yours, David. I don't want to be his anymore," she said.

David gasped as she did something he had given up asking her to do; she began to remove the wedding ring from her finger.

"It's time for me to stop wearing this. It's not just that I don't love him anymore; I love you, David. It's not fair on you."

"Will you give it back to him?" David asked.

She returned him a bitter smile, pursing her lips. "Oh, he'd love that. He'd keep it. It would be a trophy for him. Just like I was."

She turned away from David. "No. I'm not letting him have it." Her thumb and forefinger held the ring as she meditated on it. Jessica laughed. "Maybe I'll give it to our puckle! I remember you told me people used to give things to the water." Before he could protest, Jessica's arm had gone up, and she flung the ring with her full force into the mere. Two ducks that swam close to them paid no heed to the small plop, whose ripples spread out to encompass almost the whole surface of the calm pond.

"I was going to ask you if you were quite sure …" David offered quietly.

"Well it's a bit late now!" Jessica beamed, throwing herself once again into David's arms. And they kissed again, thinking of nothing but each other.

*

In retrospect, the first sign of something strange that David could recall occurred that night, when Jessica went downstairs after midnight to retrieve a pair of slippers she had left in the kitchen. When she came back to bed she reported a strange smell, "like incense, I thought it was, but not the joss-stick kind". She caught the scent as she was passing the door to the summer dining room – the Roman room – which was on the way to the kitchen.

"It was odd, because I didn't smell any incense there earlier …"

David laughed. "Who knows what Jonathan's up to!"

And he thought no more about it.

They had not managed to explore much more of the park on the previous day, so David decided they would take on the estate the next morning, walking a full circuit. Both he and Jessica enjoyed walking, even in winter, so he knew he could persuade her to spend the day beating the bounds.

Throwing open the curtains, David was disappointed to see the weather had turned; he had hoped for another fine day, but a sallow, yellowish fog lay over the landscape instead. He certainly hoped it would lift soon; it felt claustrophobic, and rather oppressive. But the best way to shake off such feelings was to walk them off, and no doubt the sun would break through. After a lavish breakfast – Jonathan's fridge was well-stocked with delicacies like oak-smoked organic bacon – they headed out across the moat bridge, but in spite of the good boots they were wearing they were soon bogged down in an extraordinary quantity of mud.

"I don't remember any rain in the night," Jessica remarked, "This is a bloody quagmire!" They regained the surface of the path leading down to the mere, now barely visible for the sheen of mud, and began to retrace their steps of yesterday. The mere was invisible in the fog, its attendant trees looming gradually out of the fog as they picked their way closer.

A man's voice, slightly muffled by the thick blanket of fog, broke the silence.

"I wouldn't go down there if I were you!"

David turned to see the stereotypical Norfolk farmer, in flat cap and padded jacket, striding towards them as quickly as the undertow of mud would allow; he seemed spattered with it almost to the waist. All he was lacking was the broken shotgun over his arm. David's first thought was that the man thought they were trespassers, and he prepared to explain himself. But the man seemed to know who they were.

"You must be Mr Gresveney's guests. My name's Townsend, I farm the land here. You might want to avoid the mere today; I've never seen so much mud in my life. It's not safe, to be honest with you. My tractor's gone and sunk into it, over by the Paddock Field."

"It's pretty odd," David observed, having exchanged pleasantries with the farmer. "We were down here yesterday, and it was fine. Was there a lot of rain in the night?"

"Not that I heard," Mr Townsend replied, "It's just this damn fog. Moisture in the air. But I can't account for this much mud. Damn strange, if you ask me. It's worse the closer you get to the mere. One of the sheep already got sucked in." Jessica put a hand over her mouth. "Oh my God, you're joking."

"No joke." Townsend shook his head. "I heard it at first light, terrible sound. I didn't get there soon enough, the mud was so thick. All I saw was the poor beast going into the mere. An odd thing, though," he paused.

"What was especially odd?" David asked.

"I've lost sheep to water, even cows. They slip down the banks, that sort of thing. But this time, the sheep wasn't slipping. It was more like – well, like the mud was moving, not the beast."

The words conjured images of B-movie horror; a moving mass of voracious mud. David felt the need to seek some sort of explanation. "A sudden surge in the water-table, maybe. Global warming and all that. Weird fluid dynamics in the mud, I suppose."

"That's as maybe. It's like nothing I've ever seen. Anyways, I need to get back to my tractor. That's the rest of my day that is, trying to get the damn thing out of the mud. No use crying over a lost sheep. I'll have to tell Mr Gresveney later."

With that, the farmer was striding away into the fog bank.

"I think I'd like to go back to the house now, David." Jessica pressed his arm. He didn't want to appear disturbed by the circumstances, but he had to agree; there was no point pursuing the walk anyway.

*

They found Jonathan reclining on a chaise-longue in the Roman dining room, dressed in a kingfisher-blue silk dressing gown of a kind that only he could somehow carry off without looking pretentious.

"I hear you met old Townsend. He texted me about that sheep. Come and have a drink."

Jonathan poured them both a sherry while they recounted their conversation with the farmer.

"It seems really odd; I just don't see where all the mud's come from."

"Well, odd or not, I suggest a day indoors; there's not much point heading out till this horrible fog lifts." Jonathan declared.

David found himself sitting opposite the fireplace, which brought the welcome comfort of a crackling flame; just the sort of cosiness he had craved at Pucklemere – even if the mosaic of the Hydra above it was hardly attractive. Interesting and incredibly skilled, to be sure, but the realism of the monster's heads seemingly lunging towards the viewer wasn't quite what David felt like admiring at that moment.

"It's not like you need to be anywhere, is it? Now," Jonathan settled back into a reclining position, "you two need to tell me all about how you met."

David yielded to Jessica the responsibility of telling the story. She was much better at that sort of thing.

"I see you've taken off the wedding ring," Jonathan observed, once Jessica had explained the complications of her divorce proceedings with Mike.

She smiled. "I threw it in the mere, actually! Yesterday, when we were down there. I just thought it was time."

The owner of Pucklemere raised an eyebrow. "A gift for the gods! Bold indeed. Ah, well – I'm sure the archaeologists can marvel at it the next time they dredge the mere."

*

Jonathan cooked them a long, leisurely lunch and they spent the afternoon in the library. David relished the opportunity to engage once more in the sort of extended, animated intellectual conversations he and Jonathan used to have as undergraduates. Jonathan was a man who had the privilege of being interested in everything, while specialising in nothing. Jessica's contributions to the conversation were more sporadic, but it was clear she enjoyed Jonathan's charming company. Time slipped almost imperceptibly away, and before they knew it, it was dark outside. Jessica offered to cook some dinner – an offer which, after the obligatory protestations, Jonathan eventually accepted.

"Let's be awfully grand and have it in the Roman dining room," Jonathan proposed.

And so it was that, by the light of Jonathan's splendid candelabra, they sat down to eat Jessica's interpretation of duck à l'orange, accompanied this time by a fine vintage of Saint-Émilion.

"Do you know, I've only just realised it's Christmas Eve," David laughed. "I can't believe it doesn't feel like it."

"Saturnalia! Let's not forget. No Christmas here." Jonathan cried. "In fact, let's raise a glass to old Saturn. To the Golden Age!"

Jonathan cheerfully joined the toast, although as he caught the heads of that damned Hydra out of the corner of his eye, seeming to twist and coil in the candlelight, he could not help recalling that Saturn also devoured his own children.

"What's that smell, Jonathan?" Jessica asked calmly. "It's quite strong, isn't it?"

Their host sniffed the air. "Damn, you're right. Smells a bit like incense."

"I smelt it last night," Jessica said. "Did you light something?"

"Me? Apart from these candles, nothing. And you wouldn't catch me with scented candles. No, I'm afraid I can't explain the incense."

"It's not *just* incense, though, is it … ?" David interjected. "Jessica, you did take all the meat out of the oven, didn't you?"

"Of course. It's all here!"

"There's a hint of, well, charred flesh. Like a barbecue, masked by incense."

The flames on the candelabra, hitherto steady, momentarily flickered as if a breeze was passing. But they felt no breeze. Then, as they gazed at the candles, the central flame slowly turned an intense green-blue.

Jonathan stood up calmly, but there was a serious note in his voice, rarely heard from someone so reliant on his charm and wit.

"I'm sorry, but I think we should probably go to a different room."

David was breathing shallowly. "You don't think – "

"I just think we should carry on the discussion elsewhere, don't you?"

Jessica was already moving towards the door. The southern end of the room, where tall sash windows and a glazed door looked out onto what remained of the old bowling green, was in darkness; but from that darkness there now came a soft sound, like sand falling on glass. Like sand; or perhaps even mud.

He was not sure how he steeled himself to turn his back on that darkness and follow Jonathan to the other end of the dining room, but he did; and once they were in the corridor Jonathan walked briskly towards the stairs. David thought he heard, but couldn't be sure, a sound of splitting glass. But Jonathan was still striding up the stairs. He didn't stop at the first floor, either, but headed to the attic and what looked like an old box room.

"The reason we're in here," Jonathan stated calmly, "Is that this room looks out over the dining room and the south lawn. And you can see the edge of the mere on the right, if you open the window and look out." He unfastened the latch as he said it, letting in the cool evening air.

"I can't really see anything," David declared, as he peered out into the darkness.

And then he saw it; silhouetted against the grass of the bowling green by the dancing light of the candles, still burning in the dining room – but whether it was inside the dining room, or outside on the terrace, he could not tell. It was a mercy he could see no more than a shadow, because that shadow was awful enough. When, in the years afterwards, he tried to describe it he kept returning to that grotesque mosaic of the Hydra; not that it was exactly the same, or that he gained any very clear impression of what it was at all; but something about the way it moved reminded him of that image. Writhing; unclean; evil in its intent.

"My God, what is it?"

"I don't know," Jonathan replied. "But I wonder if it was a good idea of yours, Jessica, to throw that ring into the mere. Did you say anything, were there any words you spoke?"

Jessica was shivering, although whether from fear or from the cold air David could not tell. "I said something; David told me about the meaning of the name, so I said I'd give my ring to the spirit of the mere, to the puckle thing."

Jonathan shook his head. He spoke quietly and quickly. "That might just be the source of the bother … David, you remember that Sir Basset drowned in the mere? There was a rumour, something the locals used to talk about

– that he when he built the Roman dining room over a Roman building, he woke something up. And we had trouble back in the '80s, too, when my father dredged the mere."

"You don't believe in this kind of stuff, do you?" David was grappling with his own incredulity.

"It's not what I believe, David; it's what it means to live alongside the past. There are things – things you need to find a way to co-exist with. Things that are best left alone. The mere is one of those things, let me tell you."

"So what the hell do we do?" Jessica sobbed now, as David tried to comfort her. "Do we just wait for that thing to come for us?"

*

They waited. For what seemed like hours, David and Jonathan took turns at the window; neither was sure what they were looking for, but somehow the open window relieved the growing sense of claustrophobia they all felt. There were old blankets in a chest in the room, and they wrapped themselves in them to stave off the cold. When at last they heard it, it was a soft sound – a creeping sort of grating on the wooden boards of the corridor, like a sledge being pulled across mud. It was approaching midnight.

And then, all of a sudden, another sound broke the silence and spilled through the window. From across the park, a peal of bells rang out from the little village church. Midnight Mass was over, and the ringers were marking Christmas Day. The bells drowned out the awful sound of the advancing horror, whatever it was; and when the peal finally fell silent, so too did everything else. It was as if the bells had cleared the air; the feeling of claustrophobic oppression was gone. Jonathan gingerly closed the window. Then he put his ear to the door. All was quiet.

They stayed in the room, of course; all David remembered was falling asleep all together, as if in a heap, while one of the chests remained pushed up against the door. But when they awoke at first light Jonathan declared his intention to go outside.

"I think we're OK. It's a thing of the night, I think."

He opened the door and stepped into the corridor, returning white-faced.

"I think you'll want to see this," he declared.

The whole corridor, up to a few feet away from the door of the box room, was clotted with semi-dried mud. Indeed, there was a trail of mud all the way through the house, leading from the broken windows of the Roman dining room, where the candles had burnt down to their sockets in the candelabra.

To The Unclean Spirits

Robin's hands were trembling gently with excitement, his elbows braced against the green Formica table top as he gesticulated towards Cassie, as if unsure that she grasped the importance of his words.

"I've got it now, Cass. This is something new. Something new on the Wall – just think of that! It's the MPhil, it's an article – hell, it's probably a book."

"Robin, I'm as excited as you are …"

Robin frowned, letting his long, freckled forearms fall across one another, his voice full of disappointment. "You don't sound it."

"It's just … I honestly don't want to discourage you – but how are we supposed to find it? After all this time? How much detail have you got, really?"

"You need to come over and see the drawings and the map for yourself." He replied firmly.

"I'm not sure …"

"Well if you want to be sure, that's the way. You're the expert eye, Cass – I know that. I trust you. But I really think this is a big one."

Cassie felt she had little choice but to agree to see the papers, at the very least. If she hadn't known better, she might have thought Robin was trying to flatter her expertise in an effort to prolong their flagging relationship. But he seemed too genuinely enthused about his discovery for that.

Nevertheless, Cassie remained convinced that she and Robin were rapidly running out of road. A basic incompatibility, that was what it was; nothing specific that she could put her finger on, and no real blame either way. She just felt uneasy, after a while, in Robin's presence. Flashes of the Robin she thought she had fallen in love with were increasingly rare; and a different Robin, with something like a paranoid streak, was showing himself all too often. Whatever it was, she knew it was best ended sooner rather than later. Hurt there would always be, but the longer she lingered, the greater the damage.

They fixed on a date for Cassie to visit Robin's mother's house. Although she and Robin had been together for almost two years, it was only her second visit – after that first, exquisitely embarrassing 'meet the parents' moment. Cassie learnt about Robin's father early on; how he had been a brilliant archaeologist, how he had gone missing all those years ago – and how the example of his father inspired Robin to study archaeology himself. The only difficulty was that, quite frankly, Robin lacked his father's brilliance. Cassie did not think there was much chance of Robin ever becoming an archaeologist, or indeed ever beginning the postgraduate study he talked about so much.

Robin simply lacked ideas. Everything about him felt – well, derivative. Even his burning ambition to study archaeology was derivative of a father he had barely known, while his desire to continue his studies felt derivative of Cassie herself, who was finishing up her PhD. It irritated her that Robin lived out his academic dreams vicariously through her; that was how it felt to her, anyway. Yet unoriginal as he was, Robin was not lacking in passion for the ideas of others, and when his mother came upon a stash of the vanished man's papers when clearing out the garage, the thought that Robin might have access to new research of his father's entirely took control of him, seemingly directing Robin's every thought.

Cassie arrived at the bungalow on a humid day in early July. The garage stood open behind an ancient beige camper van that blocked the driveway; Cassie dimly made out Robin and his mother moving in the darkness within. As when she had first met her, Robin's mother struck Cassie as prematurely old, with the mannerisms and dress of a lady in her seventies or eighties; Cassie doubted she was much older than sixty. She could barely imagine how the woman had survived her husband simply vanishing into thin air, but it was clear to Cassie that Robin's mother was the sort of self-sacrificing person who lived for her husband, then for her son. With Robin no longer at home, her life was essentially over. Cassie could barely bring herself to contemplate that awful half-life.

The newly discovered papers, yellowed, foxed and sending up a faint smell of mildew, were laid out on the polished dining table.

"We thought we had all his papers," Robin explained, "but mum found these under a sort of hatch in the middle of the garage – the one you lie down in to fix a car's chassis. She must have put them down there all those years ago because they're, er …" Robin lowered his voice, glancing towards the kitchen where his mother was busy making tea.

"They're … ?"

"They're the papers that were in the van when it was found – you know, when he went missing."

Cassie nodded. "OK, that is interesting. Did the police look at them back then?"

Robin scratched his head. "Oh God, I suppose they must have. I don't remember the investigation. You know I was only five. But they show what he was working on right before he went missing. Come on, sit down."

Robin ushered Cassie to a chair and pushed a sketch towards her. Robin's father had been a half decent archaeological draughtsman; what she saw in front of her was a technical drawing of what she instantly recognised as a Roman altar. The scale drawn alongside it suggested it was about the size of a small coffee table, inscribed in crude, sloping yet legible Roman script:

NVMINIB.
INMVNDIS
VOT.
SOLVES

"That's a nice drawing, but the inscription can't be right." Cassie said.

"OK, why?" Robin leant in to take a closer look.

"Well, an altar inscription has three basic components. We have a dedication to the deity or deities in the dative, sometimes with a title. That's obviously *numinibus inmundis* here; then the name of the dedicator, and a phrase like *votum solvit*, 'performed his vow' or something similar. This is just garbled."

"You mean it's nonsense Latin?"

"Oh it makes sense, as a sentence. But it doesn't make any sense in the context of an altar." Cassie assured Robin.

"You're sure? I mean, what does the Latin actually say? I have some idea already but I'd like to hear what you think."

Cassie smiled. "It's not very difficult Latin, and I'm sure you've got the same reading as me. *Numinibus inmundis* would be something like 'to the dirty spirits', and the rest is second person singular, in the future tense 'you will perform a vow'. You see – it just doesn't make sense."

"'Unclean', I thought. it's more of a religious word. To the unclean spirits. 'You will perform a vow to the unclean spirits'. Something like that. A bit creepy, really."

Cassie shook her head. "Not creepy, just wrong. If it's a dedication then it's going to be in the past tense – third person. And where's the name of the dedicator? And who the hell are these 'unclean spirits'? It's easily done if you're not an epigrapher or a Latinist, but your dad obviously blundered the inscription."

"So why does it still make sense? I mean, if he was crap at Latin it would just be nonsense, wouldn't it?" Robin was beginning to sound rather desperate, but Cassie was not going to budge from her professional turf.

"There are a lot of grammatical forms in Latin that will make sense. If you're unsure of the reading and you're reaching for letters, there's a reasonable probability your inscription will still make sense as *something*. That doesn't mean it's the right reading, though."

Robin sighed, then composed himself. "OK. Let's put aside the whole inscription and accuracy thing. The point is, the altar's real. But dad never recovered it. He must have found it off his own bat and drawn it *in situ*."

"You mean he wasn't part of an excavation team?"

"Mum said he had a falling out with the lead archaeologist. Went off and did his own thing. I don't think it was strictly legal."

Cassie smiled. "A different world, the nineties …"

"But look – " Robin pushed another piece of paper across the table, this time a hand-drawn map. "Here's the location. I've checked it against the OS map. It checks out, a real spot."

From then on, the conversation became difficult. Robin had a degree in archaeology – albeit not a very good one – but little experience of actually working on an excavation.

"Robin, there are protocols …" She began to explain the ethical implications of the reporting of a find, and Robin's ethical responsibility (in her view) to discuss any finds Robin's father made just before his death with the lead archaeologist of the excavation he was supposed to have been working on at the time.

Robin put his head between his tensely drawn palms. "You're talking a lot here about *my* responsibilities. I didn't find this stuff. My dad did. Then he was gone for good. If you ask me, my first responsibility is to him."

"To him, yes – to his reputation as an archaeologist. Of course he would have reported this and had it properly recorded if something hadn't happened to him –"

It was at that moment Robin's mother came back into the room.

*

Cassie was sure she would have been able to say no to Robin alone. But faced with his mother, pleading with her to find out what her husband had found all those years ago, Cassie found it impossible to refuse what she considered a ridiculous trip. Ridiculous at best, and damaging to her career at worst. To set out to find an artefact illegally excavated thirty years earlier without telling anyone was a pretty flagrant breach of archaeological ethics. But Robin's mother pleaded with Cassie to confirm it was really there before bringing in the professionals to record it; it was a matter of her husband's reputation as an archaeologist. Had he really found something new, something important? The woman's anxiety to establish the truth was understandable enough; but Robin, Cassie knew, was motivated by something else entirely. He was fixated on the idea that his father had discovered a new kind of Roman religious artefact. And that was what he needed for a research proposal; it was the kind of discovery he thought would catapult him into the world of academic archaeology.

Cassie had been to Hadrian's Wall half a dozen times, but the journey had never felt this long before. They were driving up in the same old beige camper van found abandoned near Wark-on-Tyne all those years ago – which, frankly, felt eerie; even ghoulish. Not that Cassie had much choice; the alternative was hiring another vehicle or paying for accommodation, something neither she nor Robin could afford. It was strange enough that Robin's mother had kept the camper; but as with everything else in her home, the clock stopped thirty years ago. Luckily the vehicle was still in reasonable working order, although Cassie was still reluctant to take her turn at driving it.

The weirdness of using that vehicle was one thing; the unspoken tension between her and Robin was quite another. It was always possible, Cassie reflected, that Robin was completely unaware their relationship was unravelling; stranger illusions had prevailed, after all. For Cassie, it was as though every moment of silence screamed failure back at her; her failure, Robin's failure, the dread of the inevitable conversation where she confronted him with the unvarnished truth. As they approached the outskirts of Newcastle, in a mockery of the vaunted summer, the weather took a turn for the worse. It began raining heavily. By the time they crossed the Wall, at Tower Tye, Cassie was squinting through a perpetually replenished sheen of water that coated the windscreen like a thick lense, in spite of the ineffectual wipers.

They had passed beyond the northern frontier of the Roman Empire. Low banks of cloud, pencil-lead grey, just grazed the summits of the low hills north of the Wall. Robin leant forward awkwardly over the wheel, peering through the cascade.

"It's going to be like this all week, isn't it? How are we supposed to find anything in this?" Cassie demanded, raising her voice above the hammering droplets.

Then the rain began to subside, and the black ribbon of the North Tyne became visible below the road. They turned into a long, narrow lane hemmed in by trees that finally gave way to a view of the dark brown mass of Ravensheugh Crags, rising beyond a moorland scattered with stunted and wind-blown trees. Then they were on an even narrower road, a single track rising gently towards a ridge, with a sharp series of meanders as they descended again into the valley and crossed the Gofton Burn, transformed suddenly into an angry torrent by the huge volume of rain that had fallen. As the van's engine began to complain again at another slow climb, Robin turned to Cassie.

"I think we're not too far away now," he said. "I think this is it."

He brought the camper van to a halt in front of a wooden farm gate. Two wheel-tracks ran into a field of cows. To the right, just beyond a drystone wall, an isolated cottage flew the red and yellow flag of Northumbria.

"You do realise this is someone's land, Robin? That they are actually going to notice if you take a camper van down here?"

They had spent hours, it seemed, studying the Ordnance Survey map and matching it to the hand-drawn map made by Robin's father.

"We'll be in and out. That's why I brought the van to sleep in. If they catch us we'll move it somewhere else close by. But they're not going to be coming out in this weather, are they? Now are you going to get out and open that gate or am I?"

"Seriously, Robin – this is a clapped-out eighties camper van, not a four-by-four! If you even get it up that track in the mud there's no guarantee you'll ever get it out again – " Cassie checked herself. She had let it slip from her mind that this was the spot – or somewhere close by – that the van had been found after his father's disappearance. It was unfair to argue with him when he must be going through strong emotions. But she did genuinely worry about the viability of the path.

Robin had already got out of the car, pulling up the hood of his waterproof as he hauled open the gate. A gust of wind blew a shower of raindrops into Cassie's face through the open car door. Robin slammed his door shut irritably as he climbed back into the driver's seat for the second time; and then they were lurching up the muddy track, which drew level with the cottage before taking a sharp left around a hill marked on the old hand-drawn map as Moralee. Ahead of them lay a narrow strip of woodland that, Cassie knew from the map, concealed another small burn. They were alongside the wood now; the aluminium pots and pans were clashing in the back of the van as they rocked from side to side on a track that was now barely distinguishable from the surrounding field.

Finally, Robin cut the engine. They were almost at the end of the track. He had taken care to place the van so it was screened by a couple of trees from the windows of the cottage. No guarantee that they wouldn't be seen, of course, but it was something. Robin glanced at his phone. It was already six o'clock. Cassie suggested they should eat first before heading into the wood and down to the burn.

According to Robin's father's notes, he had found the altar half covered by the roots of a tree. The roots, he thought, had somehow brought the artefact to the surface over time, or turned it over so that the inscription became visible. The archaeologist had spotted a corner of what he instantly recognised as worked stone; then he had brushed and scraped away the earth and leaves to reveal the form of the altar. There was no moving it, of course; it was too heavy for one man to lift, and in any case it was held in place by the tree's roots. He had no camera with him, so he made a sketch and then carefully re-covered the altar to protect it, marking its position tree by tree on the map he then drew for his own reference.

Neither Cassie nor Robin had the heart to try lighting the camping stove in the rain, which was still beating down hard on the roof of the van. They ate a dinner of crisps and petrol station sandwiches before Robin declared his intention to begin the search.

"Are you coming?"

"Of course." Cassie pulled on her waterproof coat and boots, although she doubted the ability of any coat to protect from the heavy splashes of Northumbrian rain that pelted her as soon as she drew back the rear door of the camper.

"Bloody hell, Robin. Are you sure? Can't we wait till the rain stops?"

"You said yourself, we need to get out of here quickly. The quicker, the better." He was armed with a high-powered torch, a trowel, and a small can of orange spray paint – with the idea of marking the way back to the altar once they located it. If, that is, they managed to find it at all.

The cover of the trees offered scant protection from the rain; they were walking on a thick mat of sopping brown bracken between a mixture of pine and deciduous trees on a steep slope above the burn, which bubbled aggressively below them under a bank of overhanging mud and weeds. Robin and Cassie spent a frustrating hour or so in the dim shade of the wood, trying to match the trees to the positions marked on the map. Robin was using a photograph of the original map on his phone, which he wiped again and again with his sleeve in an effort to keep the screen dry. But it was to no avail. Hopelessly confused and discouraged, Robin pulled down his hood and let the rain pour down over his red hair.

"It's been thirty years, for God's sake. How many of these trees have grown in that time?"

Cassie brought herself to touch his arm. "Well, maybe some of them. But let's come at it with fresh eyes tomorrow. You've just driven up the A1 for four-and-a-half hours, Robin."

With difficulty, Cassie managed to persuade Robin back into the camper van. They drew the blinds and spent the rest of the evening going over the map yet again by torchlight, this time trying to match up individual trees with photos Robin had taken on his phone. Cassie was not sure they made much progress. Around midnight they gave up and crawled into sleeping bags. Outside, the rain had stopped. Cassie lay awake for a time, listening to the other noises that now asserted themselves in the darkness: the rushing of the burn, the wind in the trees, the distant snoring of sleeping cows. At one point in the night Robin reached out to touch her; she turned sharply away from him.

*

Cassie felt like she barely slept. The van was cramped, cold even in July, and the rain continued. She could have sworn the rainwater was somehow seeping in, making everything damp. At long last she must have drifted off, as in dream she found herself standing outside in the grey light of early dawn, a blanket wrapped around her as she gazed towards the little wood. Something – or rather someone – was moving among the trees. They emerged completely without sound – diminutive, stooped figures shrouded in coarse and ragged grey mantles. Everything about them was ash-coloured; the cloaks that mercifully concealed their emaciated forms and, above all, hid their faces. The sight of their gnarled, twig-like hands was enough. In that fully-formed knowledge that accompanies dream, she knew they were *hungry*. Hunger consumed them, drove them, overwhelmed them. And as one of them reached out a crooked hand of unnatural size in her direction, she knew she could not bear them to draw any closer …

Cassie awoke in much the same grey light as the dream – damp not with rainwater, but with sweat. To her surprise, Robin was gone. Surely he couldn't have gone out searching for the altar again this early? She stepped outside into thick mud, but the rain was gone and the sun was beginning to reach through the early morning mist – it was a little after five o'clock, and a cacophony of birdsong rose from the coppice. Something, however, made Cassie unwilling to follow Robin in there, where he had surely gone, even though there was no chance of her getting lost in such a small wood. No, she would rather wait by the van, boiling up some water for tea on the camping stove.

She had already drunk two cups of tea when she became aware of someone's presence. Robin had emerged from the shade of the trees and was coming towards her. If Robin had been making Cassie uncomfortable before, for the first time since meeting him she now felt absolute revulsion toward him. Something was different, though she could scarcely place it – in the way he moved, perhaps, in his speed, or in his face. Some small alteration, barely perceptible, made him repellent to her. So much so that she stood up from the step of the van, all her instincts preparing her to turn and run. Of course, she did no such thing; it was only Robin, after all.

He did not say anything; there was a big smile on his face, although if any smile could be less reassuring, Cassie had never seen it. He was holding his phone, and as he drew close to her he held it out. It was a photograph of the altar, half buried next to the roots of a tree; the deeply incised letters were filled with moss, but Cassie could make out most of the inscription. Robin's father, it seemed, had been right.

"I found it, Cassie!" Robin exclaimed, with a glee that seemed forced.

"Wow! What time did you go out …? I'm amazed you didn't wake me up …"

"Oh, I've been out since before dawn. I couldn't wait. I climbed out through the driver's door so as not to wake you up. Then they showed me where it was."

Cassie squinted at him.

"I'm sorry, 'they'? You met someone in the wood?"

"I don't think I would ever have found it without them. I have to thank them. I – " he hesitated, as if something was caught in his throat. "I'm really sorry, Cassie. But it's really important I thank them."

Suddenly, he pushed past her and dived into the back of the van. Cassie felt as though every cell of her body screamed imminent danger. Something was very wrong. She squeezed the tin cup she was holding between her palms, and moved slowly to the side of the van. The vehicle gave a little bounce as Robin jumped down from it. The sun caught the kitchen knife he was holding in his right hand. Even though she was alert to danger, Cassie had not expected this. She knew she now risked being overtaken by the paralysis of fear, and that somehow she had to overcome any shock she felt, and simply act. There was room for nothing else.

"It's blood they want, you see; and I have to do it now, you understand – "

Lifting her foot as high as it could go, Cassie pushed the sole of her boot into Robin's stomach. He crumpled backwards as she launched herself towards the driver's door and got it open, throwing herself into the seat and reaching for the key. She had seen the mud; she knew the chances of even moving the van were thin. And the back doors were still open. But she had to try.

"Cassie!" Robin was screaming her name; then he started banging on the side of the door as if to get in – forgetting, mercifully, that the back of the van was still open. She put the vehicle into a hard reverse, hearing the wheels skidding into the deep mud. Cassie had not prayed for years; not since she was a little girl, perhaps, squeezing her eyes tight shut in a school assembly just in case she might be able to see this God that her teachers sometimes talked about. Had that been praying? In any case, she hadn't seen anything; and her mother assured her God was just a fairytale people told themselves to feel better about life. But she found her lips moving, saying something. "Please, God! Please!"

With a hard jolt that sent her bouncing in her seat and slammed the back doors shut, the van rolled out of the rut and began to move; by some miracle, when she came out of reverse it carried on moving, taking Cassie over the muddy expanse of grass towards the field gate. In her mirror she caught a view of Robin; he just stood there, making no attempt to follow, even though she could barely move the van above jogging pace. And then he did it. He held out the knife dramatically; there was a spurt of red, and he fell to the ground, face forward. She stopped the van, incredulous. It was over. They had got what they wanted.

The Green Girl

The taxi driver had been silent since realising, on the outskirts of Bury St Edmunds, that Elinor had no desire to discuss the town's traffic congestion. So his sharp intake of breath, as they turned into the village of Woolpit, took her by surprise.

"Well, well. You wouldn't see me driving that."

Elinor, absorbed in her own thoughts, had missed whatever the man was commenting on.

"Driving what?"

"Did you see that taxi? Bright green!"

"Is that not allowed or something?" Elinor had not noticed whether all the local taxis now had a standard livery.

The taxi driver raised his voice slightly, as if explaining to an imbecile. "*Green*. It's unlucky, love. I've never known a driver want a green taxi. But I suppose they don't know, do they? Indians, and that – "

Elinor interrupted the driver quickly, fearing the conversation might veer in a xenophobic direction. "How interesting. Do you often drive out here?"

"Yeah, the odd pick up now and again. Quite a big village." Elinor glimpsed the impressive medieval church festooned with yellow finials, whose spire marked the village's skyline on the A14. It was not long before the car pulled up in front of Dorothy Clyne's very lovely cottage: timber-framed, dark pink, and close to the edge of the village. After paying the superstitious taxi driver, Elinor was left in the quiet shade of the cottage, partially overgrown with pale violet wisteria.

Elinor doubted she had seen Dorothy Clyne for twenty years. Dorothy seemed ancient even then, when Elinor was a child; she remembered a kind, wrinkled face and a gentle voice, and that she let Elinor sit on the red tartan blanket that covered her thin legs. Elinor's mother had passed her telephone number to Dorothy a few days ago, telling Elinor that the old woman was keen to get in touch about something important. "It's about history, you see."

When Elinor did finally hear Dorothy's voice at the other end of the telephone, physically weak but strong in resolution, the old woman was eager to clarify – before anything else – that Elinor now worked on medieval manuscripts.

"Yes; twelfth century, mainly."

"That's wonderful. Yes, exactly right. I was wondering if you could take a look at something."

"A manuscript?"

"No, it's not that exactly. You'll have to see when you come over. Could you come over, do you think?"

A trip to Suffolk was not a completely unappealing prospect to Elinor, even if it meant staying with her mother. She readily agreed, although she tried to extract a little more information from Dorothy.

"It's just that it might not be what I think it is. I just want you to take a look at it. I don't want to, you know, claim anything that I can't back up. But I think it might be rather important. I'd just prefer you saw it before I say anything else."

A brief tap on the oak with the cast iron knocker soon summoned Dorothy, whose stoop was much more pronounced now than Elinor remembered; her tiny frame tottered alarmingly as Elinor followed her into the house, but the old woman was smiling broadly and seemed delighted to welcome a visitor. Dorothy ushered Elinor into a pleasantly cool interior where the walls were lined entirely with books. The familiar and comforting aroma of old print immediately put Elinor at ease, even when Dorothy greeted her with reference to her mother.

"I'm just so delighted Elizabeth's daughter is such a fine scholar!"

"You're very kind …"

Dorothy fussed over her visitor, practically pushing her into an ancient velvet chaise longue half piled with papers, before demanding her preferences in hot drinks. Elinor asked simply for a glass of water.

"I'm so glad you agreed to come," Dorothy declared, once she herself was clutching a cup of tea in an ancient armchair heaped with patchwork blankets. "I know I must have sounded awfully strange on the telephone; it's just – well, I've been burnt before. People around here do care an awful lot about their history, you know, and rumours sometimes spread before anything's even been confirmed, especially when it comes to something like this."

"Like this?"

"There's a local story; you probably know it. The Green Children of Woolpit."

Elinor smiled. It was a story she had first heard as a small child – a strange tale from the Middle Ages, about a green boy and girl who were found by reapers in a hole or a ditch near the village. The children could eat nothing but green food, and the boy died, but the girl lived, eventually lost her green colour, and learnt English, finally revealing that she and her brother had become lost in their own subterranean country of perpetual twilight; they had followed the sound of bells until they found themselves in our world. It was a haunting story, told and re-told many times, and perhaps the best-known of all Suffolk tales.

"Of course! Don't tell me you've found something new?"

Elinor knew well that there were only two medieval sources containing the story of the Green Children, both chronicles, and both written by monks. Dorothy shifted uncomfortably in her seat, grinning nervously.

"Well, it's actually possible that I have, yes."

Elinor's eyes widened. "A new medieval source?"

"If it's really what I think it is, then yes. The thing is …" Dorothy hesitated, then began babbling fast: "I don't have the original document; I only have an old type-written copy. It's supposed to be part of the *Collectanea Buriensia* – a whole lot of snippets of Bury documents assembled by Sir James Burrough in the eighteenth century – they're in the Record Office in Bury, but if this document was ever part of the collection it's not there now, and I've asked the Record Office and they don't know, and they have no record of it …"

Elinor knew of this collection. She tried to speak slowly and reassuringly.

"Dorothy, it's more than likely something has gone astray from the *Collectanea*; they used to be in St James's Parish Library, didn't they?"

Dorothy nodded.

"And is there an itemised catalogue of the collection from that time?"

"I don't think so …"

"Well there you are. It certainly could be."

"But without confirmation …"

Elinor leant forward and placed her palm gently on the older woman's fragile forearm. "Let's … look, shall we? Before we discuss anything else."

Dorothy nodded weakly. "Yes. Yes, of course. You must see it."

She reached over to a table covered with a stained Victorian damask cloth for a plain brown archival file, tied with string wound around a little disc of card. There were a number of very old typed pages inside, yellow and brittle with age, which Elinor thought must date from the early twentieth century – perhaps before the First World War. Dorothy carefully placed the open file in Elinor's waiting hands.

"These were given to me by the village history society, for safekeeping," she said. "They belonged to an old rector of Woolpit, but goodness only knows where he got them. They're not signed anywhere. Nobody could read the document because it's in Latin. But I think I've managed to get the gist of it."

Medieval Latin was no trouble for Elinor, who quickly made sense of the short document, which was entitled *De Sancta Maria de Wulpet*, 'About St Mary of Woolpit'. In addition to the Green Children, Woolpit was famous in the Middle Ages as a shrine of Christ's mother – the second most important Marian shrine in East Anglia, some said, after the famous 'Holy House' at Walsingham. But Elinor also knew that historians understood little of the origins of Woolpit as a shrine of the Virgin – certainly there was no story about a dream or a vision, as there was at Walsingham. She was curious indeed to see what this document had to say, and began to read:

Regnante Henrico primo ac Anselmo pontificante, apud Wulpet non longe a civitate Sancti Edmundi, messores in tempore messis ad quidem puteum (qui puteum Sancti Martini vocabatur) in fossa conveniebant ut biberent, ubi figuras pueri et puelle aeneas, viridi colore et gentilium arte factas invenisse. Quoniam messis uberrimum fuit, rustici superstitiose has figuras juxta puteum venerabantur, consentiente capellano huius loci, nomine Jacobus de Livermer, qui errorem vicanum permisit. Vicani figuras viridos pueros appellabant, et idolis gratias reddebant pro omnibus felicitatibus; sed paulatim figura pueri evanuit, vel forte vel per judicium Dei; ergo figura puelle modo in loco remansit, ubi idolici honores accepti sunt. Fabula vulga a rusticis narrabatur, qui a multis adhuc creditur, videlicet duos pueros olim viventes fuisse, et de terra emergissent. Sed Anselmus abbas, vir prudens, de fedo cultu demonis audiens, Jacobum capellanum ad se arcessivit; et predictus capellanus, peccatum idolatrie gemitu confitens, seipse abbato pro penitentia submisit. Et Anselmus, qui ad Beatum Mariam Virginem maxime devotus est, puteum sacrum Beate Virginis esse decrevit; ergo locus qui antequam demonibus consecratus esset in honorem matris Dei nunc votus est; et virescebat in loco ubi viridam puellam antequam colebatur cultus Virginis, virtute vitium vincente.

Having read through the text once, Elinor began to translate aloud as Dorothy sat back, her eyes closed. Above the mantlepiece, a cuckoo clock struck three o'clock:

"When Henry I was king, and Anselm was bishop – "

"Abbot." Dorothy corrected.

"When Anselm was abbot, at Woolpit, not far from the town of St Edmund, harvesters in time of harvest used to come to a certain well in a ditch (which was called St Martin's Well) so that they might drink; where they found figures, made of bronze, of a boy and a girl, green in colour and of Gentile – no, of *pagan* workmanship."

Elinor looked up. "Figures? Are these statues? Statues of a green boy and girl?"

"Keep reading." Dorothy insisted. Elinor returned to the text.

"Since the harvest was very fruitful, the country people superstitiously venerated these figures next to the well, with the chaplain of the place consenting, who was called James de Livermere, who permitted the error of the villagers. The villagers used to call the figures the green children, and thanked the idols for all good fortunes; but after a little while the figure of the boy disappeared, either by chance or by the judgement of God; therefore only the figure of the girl remained in the place, where it received idolatrous honours. A common fable was told by the villagers, which is still believed by many; that is, that the two children were once living, and had emerged from the earth. But Abbot Anselm, a prudent man, hearing of the filthy cult of the demon, summoned the chaplain to him; and the aforesaid chaplain, confessing with a groan the sin of idolatry, submitted himself to the abbot for penance. And Anselm, who was greatly devoted to the Blessed Virgin Mary, decreed the well to be sacred to the Blessed Virgin. Therefore, the place that beforehand had been consecrated to demons was now devoted to the honour of the mother of God; and the cult of the Virgin grew green where before the green girl was worshipped, with virtue overcoming vice."

Elinor paused when she had finished reading, feeling and examining the paper she held, as if it might be coaxed into giving up the secret of its origin. The Latin prose was plausibly twelfth-century, the orthography was medieval, and the few historical details alluded to were correct. But beyond that, in the absence of any provenance or a reference to the original document, it was hard to say what value the document had. Dorothy broke the silence.

"I'm so grateful to you, my dear," she said, "I had the general idea of the meaning but I wasn't sure. You've confirmed what I thought."

"What was that?"

"That the statues were Roman relics, I suppose – a bronze boy and a bronze girl, life-size by the sound of it. Left in the ground like that, they would have been completely green when the reapers dug them out. Maybe they were something to do with Roman well-worship at the spring. You know where the spring is?"

"East of the church somewhere – I've never actually seen it." Elinor admitted.

"Yes, the Lady's Well; it's in some woods at the end of the road. There's a moated site, but it's all covered with trees now, and the well cover is in the dried-up moat somewhere. But the Chapel of the Virgin was in the churchyard. Do you know, it had occurred to me before – before I read the document, that is – that when they called it the Lady's Well it's not altogether clear who the lady is – whether she's the Virgin, or perhaps the green girl."

A thought struck Elinor. "Well, there are plenty of cases where a saint took over from a goddess – just look at Buxton, up in Yorkshire, where Arnemetia, the goddess of the spring, became St Anne!"

Dorothy nodded. "It makes a lot of sense. But that's not really enough, is it? Not enough to make the story true." Elinor looked down at the fraying Persian carpet at her feet.

"I'm afraid that without the original document, or at least a reference to it, this isn't much to go on."

Dorothy looked terribly downcast; so much so that Elinor acceded, finally, to the old woman's offer of a cup of tea.

"One thing that does strike me, though," Elinor added, as Dorothy shakily handed her a cup and saucer, "is that the source says nothing about what happened to the statue of the green girl. We hear that the statue of the green boy was lost – which inspired, I suppose, the part of the story where the boy dies young. But in a document like this, where we hear about the priest's contrition, I'd also expect some sort of destruction of the image."

"Unless, of course, the green girl statue actually *became* the Virgin," Dorothy offered. "The statue could have been painted, re-clothed, even encased in wood. It happened elsewhere – pagan images modified for Christian worship."

Elinor laughed. "That would be extraordinary, if we had any evidence! I don't suppose we know what happened to the image?"

"There's no description of it, but people left rings, necklaces and jewels to adorn the image in their wills – even a sceptre for the Virgin to hold in her hand."

*

Elinor enjoyed that afternoon in Dorothy Clyne's company much more than she had expected; and the strange copy of a lost medieval document was indeed intriguing. But it seemed likely it would join her collection of interesting but unconfirmable curiosities – those oddities that any delver in medieval manuscripts encounters from time to time, but for want of information or context never make it as far as an article. The antiquaries of the past would no doubt have had few scruples in publishing such snippets, but Elinor knew the damage a shaky source could do to a modern historian's reputation.

Elinor had almost forgotten the affair of the Green Children manuscript when, a few weeks later, she received a call from an almost breathless Dorothy Clyne, whose voice sounded thin and far away on her antiquated landline.

"Something's been found, you see; it hasn't been made public yet, but it's being studied and catalogued in Bury. A head."

"A head? Do you mean to say it could be … ?"

"It's bronze, yes, and they think Roman. It could be her – it could be the green girl."

So here it was. Confirmation, in material form, of that mysterious twelfth-century source. Elinor anticipated a good deal of media interest in the story, in the local press at least. The Green Children were still a well-known story locally, and people were always eager for new theories to explain them – albeit usually ones that involved living, breathing children rather than bronze statues. But if a plausible case could be made that the image of Our Lady of Woolpit was somehow wholly or partly a re-adaptation of a Roman statue, it would be a major historical and archaeological discovery.

Elinor soon found herself back at the railway station in Bury St Edmunds, walking this time to the old museum on the marketplace. She had already emailed the curator for permission to see the new find, explaining that she was investigating sources about the image of Our Lady of Woolpit. He was only too willing to let her see it, although he explained that the Parochial Church Council was eager to wait for official assessments before any announcement was made. The head had been found during routine repairs, concealed in a wall cavity in the priest's room above Woolpit church's famous porch; it was astonishing, he said, that no-one had ever recovered it before. It was badly corroded, however, and might easily have been discarded as rubbish by a less-than-careful observer.

In a back room at the museum, the curator produced a Perspex box and carefully lifted the lid; there, on a shaped piece of foam, lay the exquisitely fragile head of a girl. The corroded bronze, no thicker than an eggshell, preserved the structure of the head, while the girl's mouth and a single eye survived, as well as hints of the girl's gathered up hairstyle. The gaping holes in the bronze were like oceans on a globe, voids that nonetheless somehow allowed the imagination to complete the now partial features of the almost-vanished girl. And the colour of the blemished bronze was vividly, almost preternaturally *green*; greener than any old bronze Elinor thought she had ever seen. She could not restrain herself from a sharp intake of breath at the sight. This was a fine Roman bronze, comparable in quality to the celebrated gilded head of the goddess Sulis Minerva at Bath.

"So what were they doing with a Roman antique in medieval Woolpit?"

The curator nodded. "That's the question we're asking. The archaeologists need to investigate the context, obviously – that will hopefully give us some idea of when the thing was hidden."

Elinor wondered for a moment if she should mention the type-written manuscript to the curator, but really she had no right to do so. It was Dorothy Clyne's discovery to share, if the old woman so chose. That night Elinor rang Dorothy and described the head to her.

"I suppose I'll see it if it comes to Woolpit – that's what the rector's talking about, some sort of exhibition. I don't do much travelling around these days, even as far as

Bury. But Elinor – do you think it's her? Do you think it's the green girl?"

Elinor paused, breathing deeply. "I want to say it is, of course I do. The discovery inside the church – that's a strong indication it was concealed at the Reformation, and that in turns points to a re-purposed Roman statue. It would be an astonishing discovery. But the problem is, we still can't verify that old type-written manuscript."

Dorothy sounded sad. "I agree, dear. We can't afford to share anything about our friend James de Livermere just yet. But it's not just the lack of corroboration. If it is her, if it's that statue, it doesn't feel altogether – well, right. For it to be put back in the church in public view, that is. After all, didn't the parishioners fall into idolatry?"

Elinor smiled. "Well, that's if the green girl didn't just become the Virgin. After all, that porch wasn't built until centuries after James de Livermere's time."

"There are two stories here, aren't there?" Dorothy reflected. "The green girl became the Virgin; she became the image honoured in that chapel at the well. Or there were some people in the village who clung on to the idolatry, maybe for centuries; and they hid part of the statue in that priest's room over the porch."

Dorothy's astute observation haunted Elinor's mind over the next few weeks, as she continued to ponder what to do with that stray narrative supposedly lost from James Burrough's *Collectanea Buriensia*; yes, if the document was indeed real there were two possible stories, both of them equally remarkable. But both, too, were equally unconfirmable. Elinor knew that releasing the document, especially now, would be the height of irresponsibility for a historian. The local press would seize upon it as an explanation for the Roman bronze head found in Woolpit church – already a source of much wonder and speculation – with no regard for questions of authenticity, provenance or corroboration.

Even without access to the source, the local papers lost no time in elaborating explanations of their own. Dorothy sent Elinor a cutting from the *Bury Mercury* that only strengthened her resolve that it would be wrong to share the narrative:

ROMAN TREASURE: UNIQUE 'GREEN GIRL' RETURNS TO WOOLPIT

A valuable bronze head found in a wall in Woolpit church in July is returning to Woolpit church this week after conservation at Moyse's Hall Museum and the British Museum, on special loan from Moyse's Hall where the head will eventually be permanently displayed. Nicknamed 'the green girl' after the famous story of the Green Children of Woolpit, the small bronze head of a young girl has been dated by archaeologist Professor Frances Pytts to the Roman period.

'The big mystery is why we have part of a Roman statue in a wall built in the fourteenth century,' said Prof. Pytts. 'It's a unique discovery, I don't know of anything else like it.'

Local people have been quick to suggest their own explanations, with some suggesting the Roman statue was worshipped in secret by pagans who gathered in the room above the church porch (where the statue was discovered) to worship a goddess represented by the statue.

When we spoke to historian Dr Francis Young, who has written many books about the history of Suffolk, he disagreed:

'I'm afraid there weren't any pagans in the Middle Ages, in spite of what people may think. It's far more likely that the bronze head was discovered much later – perhaps dug up by someone who didn't know what to do with it, or discarded by an antiquary or a collector.'

Whatever the truth, Woolpit's unique green girl will be on display in a special exhibition in Woolpit church from next Saturday. Admission is free, with donations kindly requested towards the maintenance of St Mary's church.

Elinor found herself smiling nervously at the irony of the journalists – and, presumably, the people of Woolpit – nicknaming the bronze head 'the green girl'. Of course, that was all it was; a nickname. No-one actually thought there was a connection between the bronze head and the story, not least because the story was twelfth-century and the head was Roman. But the serendipity of the green head of a girl being found in a place famous for its Green Children seemed to have encouraged local people to take the girl to their hearts. Elinor knew she owed Dorothy Clyne another visit, and she was curious to see the bronze head *in situ* at its exhibition. This time she did not go to Dorothy's house, but met her at a little giftshop next to the church which served tea and cake called the Elm Tree Gallery.

"I don't know how long the museum will let the church keep it," Dorothy said, "as they've had no end of problems with the exhibition," the old woman observed as she cradled a small cup of coffee between tiny, blue-veined hands.

Elinor was curious. "What sort of problems?"

"Well, false alarms in the main … the head is in some sort of special cabinet, all alarmed and so on. The alarm shouldn't go off unless someone tried to break the glass, or jemmy the case, or so the rector said. But it's been going off almost every night, and when the security firm have turned up they've found everything in order – except last night, apparently, when they found some of the exhibition boards had fallen over. But those were pretty flimsy to begin with."

"That's odd. Perhaps it was a flaw in the design of the cabinet, or the way it's alarmed."

"They've checked, apparently, and the security firm and the museum people say it's all fine. And the rector had a go at shaking the whole thing as hard as possible to see if it would go off, and it didn't."

Elinor took a sip of her peppermint tea. "And how do you think local people are feeling about the head?"

Dorothy did not answer, glancing down to her cup and then gazing up, anxiously, into Elinor's eyes.

"It's such a small thing, Elinor, and I've no doubt an old woman like me is going loopy, but … but no, I shouldn't say it."

"Go on, please do." Elinor prompted her.

"Since the exhibition's been there, it's felt odd to be in church. Something hasn't felt quite right, somehow. And I've been going to church there since I was a girl, the best part of eight decades. I've heard some strange sermons and seen some odd gimmicks from rectors, but this feels like something else. It's as though, with her there, everything feels faltering. There's no confidence in anything the rector says, there's no conviction in the words. It almost feels like we're trying to talk underwater; we can see mouths moving, but the effect isn't there. And the light, too – the light hasn't been right. You know it's a lovely bright church, at least when the sun's shining. But whenever I've been in church the shadows have been wrong – it's difficult to explain, and there's nothing there when I look straight at it, but it's as if something is flitting about, a sort of shadow, and I keep catching it out of the corner of my eye."

Before Elinor left, Dorothy insisted they pay a visit to the church together to see the bronze head. The old woman walked so slowly, supported on two sticks, that Elinor found herself wobbling slightly as she tried to keep pace.

"Do you believe in ghosts, Elinor?" Dorothy asked, as they approached the lychgate.

Elinor answered honestly. "I've never seen one. But so many people tell stories about seeing them, they can't all be lying, can they? But who really knows what they saw?"

Dorothy shook her head. "I know, I know. And that's exactly what I say to myself. Who knows what I really saw. But there are certain kinds of movement, certain ways of moving, that suggest – well, a personality. I could have sworn it was someone who was flitting about the church as a shadow, not just some trick of the wind, or the light. And I couldn't help wondering if – well, if it was him; our James de Livermere."

"I'm not sure I understand." They had reached the porch, with its magnificent niches and coats of arms fashioned from biscuit-hued yellow stone.

"Well he repented, didn't he; but he was responsible for allowing the idolatry of the green girl. And now we've brought her back. Not as the Virgin Mary she became, but as that thing of pagan workmanship – that thing they thought was so real that the stories turned her and her brother into real children with green skin. I'm not sure he wants it. And it could be that he's causing the trouble with the alarms, and all that."

Elinor had no idea what to think of this. Certainly, Dorothy wasn't the kind of woman to prattle endlessly about supernatural atmospheres and ghosts. Her conviction that something was not quite right, that something was 'off' about an intensely familiar place, seemed more chilling than any report of a chain-rattling apparition. But before she had had a chance to consider her reply they were inside the church, inching their way towards the display case. There she was: the green girl, staring out towards them from her single eye, lit from above with a bright spotlight. Once again, Elinor was struck by the intense *greenness* of the bronze. Around the case stood a number of explanatory boards bearing such texts as 'A ROMAN TREASURE' and 'A MEDIEVAL MYSTERY'. One of them even bore an artist's impression of a medieval priest, tonsured and dressed in a grey cloak, bending down to place the bronze head in a niche in the wall. His face was hidden from the viewer.

It was at this moment that Elinor caught something out of the corner of her eye, just as Dorothy had described. A shift in the proportion of light and shadow; not much, but enough to suggest *presence*. It seemed to move in the direction of the pulpit; and for a moment – not more than a blink of an eye – Elinor felt sure she discerned the outline of a man's profile against one of the pillars. A trick of the light, perhaps. No, certainly a trick of the light. But the point about tricks is that they are played deliberately. The thought provided no reassurance.

*

As it happened, the rector and the museum between them agreed to end the exhibition early; the constant call-outs of the security company were costing them both too much. So it was that the bronze head returned to Moyse's Hall, and tranquillity to St Mary's church. Elinor felt unexpectedly moved, a few months later, when her mother rang to tell her Dorothy Clyne was dead. The memory of that strange conversation, in which Dorothy confessed her belief that James de Livermere was unhappy about the presence of the green bronze girl, had stayed with her. But Elinor still felt guilty that she had done nothing to follow up the original document on which the typewritten account of the green statues might have been based.

"I don't suppose you know what happened to all her papers? She had a very interesting collection of snippets on local history and folklore." Elinor asked her mother.

"Do you know, that's the funny thing! I never thought Dorothy would do something like that, but they found all her papers as a pile of ash in her back garden."

Defixio

"It's untranslated?"

The Professor carefully removed the little box from the shelf and opened it, to reveal a tiny, irregular square of lead with faintly visible scratches on it.

"Yes. Never published. It's a bit of a tragic story, actually. The chap who was translating it – Paul Foster, quite a brilliant guy – he drowned in the Cherwell. There was an inquest, but they never determined if he took his own life or whether it was just an accident. That was thirty years ago – I'd only just started tutoring at Balliol."

James carefully received the box from the Professor and scrutinised the curse tablet.

"And this is one of the *defixiones* from Pucklemere?"

The Professor nodded. "Yes, in west Norfolk. Dredged from the mere there in '87, I think it was. It was some sort of water shrine. There were a couple of other tablets, but they were blank or indecipherable. Paul told me he'd made a transcription of this one, though; but after his death no-one could find it – although he'd burnt some of his papers on the stove in his digs, oddly enough."

"So you never saw the transcription?"

The Professor sighed. "No, sadly not. It's always a pain to have to reinvent the wheel, but if you do want to study this one you'll need to start from scratch, I'm afraid."

It was an extraordinary opportunity. James was well aware that the vast majority of curse tablets found in Britain had, after painstaking effort, been transcribed and translated. He had plenty of ideas on the reinterpretation of the known tablets, but he had never anticipated that his DPhil might include a previously unpublished *defixio*.

The Professor grinned. "Well, if you're game I'll get the photography department to take some high res images and you can take it from there."

A few days later the files came through by email; James inwardly gave thanks that he did not, like Paul Foster, have to spend days in the Ashmolean with a magnifier studying the artefact itself. The photographer had taken numerous images, including some with a high-powered lamp directed across the surface of the *defixio* to better reveal the scratches of Roman cursive. It was a notoriously difficult script – looking, to the untrained eye, like little more than a series of short parallel lines, slightly off the perpendicular; it was, after all, a script for writing with a stylus on wax, on bark, or – in this case – on soft lead. There was no punctuation and often – as in this case – no obvious spaces between words. James knew, however, that curse tablets were often formulaic, and there was a large published corpus of the inscriptions from throughout the Roman Empire. He set to work, therefore, with a confidence that was perhaps unwarranted.

By the time the light was beginning to fade in his Jericho room, and the glare of the laptop starting to irk his eyes, James had begun to think he might not be up to the task, and even to contemplate the unpleasant possibility that this curse tablet might be one of the exceptions – not another formulaic example, where the major challenge was the transcription of personal names that might well be unique

British words, but a wholly unusual type of *defixio* – perhaps even like a couple of the tablets pulled out of the goddess Sulis Minerva's spring at Bath that seemed to be in a language other than Latin – presumably the lost language of the ancient Britons. He remembered something the Professor once said to him – that curse tablets were never meant to be read, at least by humans. If it was something so unusual, James was hardly equal to the task; he would have to hand the whole thing over to some Celticist. The possibility of including the tablet in his DPhil thesis, except as a footnote, would be lost.

Sighing at the prospect, he closed his laptop and made his way through the darkening streets to the lights of St Giles, where he skipped across the lanes of traffic to the Lamb and Flag. There was usually someone in there he knew, but as he scanned the bar this evening his eyes met with Alyssa's, sipping cider with a group of friends by the soot-stained ancient fireplace. She and James had been undergraduates together, although at the time they hardly knew each other. But in the first year of their respective DPhil studies they became friends. More than friends, hazily, on one occasion – and to James's regret, because Alyssa now exercised a kind of fascination over him that he dearly wished she did not. Not that he was in love with her – there had never been anything quite like that – but she was someone he could never say no to. A kind of chaotic energy, a disruptive influence. Once they had made eye contact, he knew she would come over; either that, or he would be compelled to come over to her.

It did not come to that, and at a lull in the conversation Alyssa joined him at the bar.

"I see you're back in the land of the living, James. Are you going to buy me a drink?"

He did so, of course.

"Still studying magic?" she asked.

He smiled. "That makes me sound like some sort of wizard. I'm studying the palaeography of Roman Britain and reinterpreting some of the corpus of sources."

"All your sources are magic, though, aren't they?"

"They happen to be curse tablets; you know they are."

"But you still won't accept them as magic. Interesting."

Alyssa was studying something to do with literary theory – James was never quite sure what, and at this point it felt embarrassing to ask.

"Do you believe in magic, James?" she now asked.

James glanced quickly around the bar, as if to check none of his fellow students or researchers were assessing his answer.

"I suppose the mind can be very powerful; that's a kind of magic, I suppose. I mean, if someone wrote my name on a curse tablet and threw it into the Cherwell offering me to evil gods, and then told me they'd done it – I'd probably be bricking it, wouldn't I? It's classic psy-ops. You see how it works in Africa, with witch doctors and all that."

Alyssa took a sip of white wine. "You haven't really answered my question, though."

"Haven't I? I'm saying that if someone cursed me, I'd be disturbed by that. It's not that I'd be certain it was real – being threatened with a curse isn't like being threatened with a loaded gun. It's the uncertainty, I suppose. It's probably bunkum, but there's that sliver of doubt – and with a curse, I suppose it's the sliver of doubt that gets you."

Alyssa nodded. "I'm impressed. You have thought about this."

"Why, did you think I was just a transcription monkey?"

"No; I'm just glad you've made the effort to get into the heads of the people who made your curse tablets. And I think you're right. Uncertainty is magic's domain. There are the people who are certain about magic, who make it into a kind of religion; and there are the rationalists, the ones who refuse to even contemplate it. But most of us are in the middle. We don't believe in it, but we can still fear it. It's part of magic's mad logic."

James was glad he and Alyssa could find something to agree on.

"I'm working on one right now, actually – completely untranscribed and unstudied. It was just sitting there in the Ashmolean. Someone was translating it in the eighties but died suddenly before he could finish it."

"Uh oh!" Alyssa grimaced.

James shook his head wearily. "Yes, yes; it's a great story, the curse tablet that curses you and all that. But the poor guy drowned in the river apparently. I'm not sure it's very respectful to be weaving gothic fantasies about him."

"But you have to admit – it's a bit of a horror cliché. Everyone who reads the tablet dies." She grinned mischievously.

"I think at this point I'll die trying to read it, let alone unleash something by actually succeeding. It's bloody difficult." James stared into his empty glass.

"Well, I can't help you there. I never was much good at palaeography or epigraphy. But I'm not sure I'd want to be you. There's always that question-mark, isn't there?"

James appreciated Alyssa's imagination – she was always a lot of fun to talk to, willing to say things others wouldn't. But he was feeling tired out, and made his excuses.

*

The breakthrough came about a week later, when James was working late in the college library. The transcription process had been all consuming; even in his dreams, James found himself tracing the strokes of the stylus like a much-studied map. In one dream he even found himself dropped, flea-sized, onto the rough surface of the *defixio*; the scratches were now deep grooves in the ground that his feet followed as if tracing a path through a labyrinth. But meaning stubbornly refused to stick. Like those early Victorian attempts at photography, James found he could create impressions of meaning by imposing a structure on the letters he thought he'd got right … but within minutes the image faded; there was nothing to fix it, no overarching structure of understanding what the text might be saying. And after a few more letters, it became clear the text said nothing like what he had imagined. Yet by the time he took his seat in the library that afternoon he was sure of one thing; the text was Latin, and not British, Gaulish or some other language.

When the breakthrough came, it was as though everything in an unfocussed and jumbled picture swam into view. It felt almost … well, like magic. Perhaps, thought James, because his unconscious mind had been training his conscious and the two were finally ready to begin a fruitful partnership. Not only did it become clear to James what the text said, but he also began to anticipate what it might say next. And he was broadly right. It was a thrilling sensation; the kind of excitement that had drawn him into research in the first place. As for the text itself, it was short – there were a number of abbreviations but, assuming he was right about the expansion of those, he was looking at last at a full transcription of the text:

Ego Ventonaurus, quem peperit Silvicola, divo Nodenti omnes trado quos me aliquam iniuriam fecerunt; in abyssum caderent, vel fures, vel proditores, vel adulteri, vel lectores horum sacrosanctorum verborum inter me et te; a tenebris sequantur in omnibus viis usque ad mortem. Ergo oro, precor, rogo vos o Nodente deus chai, rem hanc fac in perpetuum per omne aevum.

I Ventonaurus, whom Silvicola bore, give to the god Nodens all those who have done me any injury; may they fall into the abyss, whether thieves, or betrayers, or adulterers, or readers of these inviolable words between me and you. May they be pursued by shadows in all their ways unto death. Therefore I beg, I pray, I ask you o Nodens, god of Chaos, do this thing in perpetuity through all ages.

It was a pretty striking curse; and James smiled at the fact that the text did, in fact, target anyone who read it, just as Alyssa had imagined. That was a feature he'd never seen before.

Although James's first instinct was to rush out of the library and try to find the Professor in order to tell him all about the discovery, he considered that his supervisor would probably be more impressed if the basic editorial work on the inscription were done first. There would be more to do in the coming days on variant interpretations of the abbreviations, but James was now as sure as he could be that he had a plausible and, in his view, correct reading. He would also need to work with an archaeological illustrator to produce a scaled line drawing of the tablet that included his interpretation of the text; but all of that lay in the future. For now, he just needed something good enough to show the Professor, and the adrenalin of the discovery fuelled him late into the night. The library was completely empty by nine o'clock, although oddly James had the feeling he was not alone. A couple of times he thought he caught movement out of the corner of his eye in the darkness of the stacks on either side of him, or even something over his shoulder; but it could have been a bird or a bat flying past the window.

It was just before midnight when he finally packed up his laptop and, still buoyed with elation at his discovery, began the walk home. It was cold outside, and central Oxford was almost deserted; he passed a few knots of drunk students, even on a Tuesday night; and someone always seemed to keep pace about a hundred yards behind him. He glanced behind him a couple of times, but the figure fell into the patches of dimness between the streetlights and remained persistently obscure.

*

The next morning James's first appointment was with the Professor. As he passed through a dark arch – one of the longer ones connecting two quads – he could have sworn that a figure standing in the shadows reached out as if to grab him. There was no-one there when he looked back, of course – just a silly imagining, but it shook James a little. The Professor was, of all places, in the college chapel; he had explained in the email that he liked to listen to the organist practising on Wednesday mornings. And he was a fellow of the college so senior that eccentricities of this kind went unquestioned.

James felt oddly relieved as he crossed the threshold of the chapel. A vague feeling of being followed, which had been dogging him since his walk home last night and had even continued in his dreams of the night before, suddenly evaporated – and by doing so, made him more aware that it had been there in the first place. The organ was playing some lugubrious chorale by Buxtehude and the Professor was seated in one of the stalls, leaning forward with his eyes closed while his fingers delicately interlaced in rapt listening. James felt bad about interrupting him – but, on the other hand, that was where he had told his student to meet him. He heard James approaching and opened his eyes, motioning to the parch of oak bench beside him.

"James! Come and take and seat."

"I've brought my transcription – " he began removing a file to show the Professor, who motioned it away, tutting.

"James, James; let's take this slowly. I'm delighted you think you have a text. But this is not how we proceed. This business isn't about "Eureka" moments and discoveries. When I was translating I would often have dozens of different possible transcriptions of a single tablet, pinned around the house to study for weeks. There's always ambiguity."

"I was really struggling, I admit – but I had the most astonishing moment of clarity last night – it all came together."

The Professor shook his head. "Moments of clarity? I'd say those are the moments to be avoided. The mind plays tricks on us, James, especially when the brain is so intently focussed on one problem. There aren't many of us who can do this, as well you know; and there's a great deal of pressure because if you can't transcribe it, who can? That kind of pressure can turn the mind; it can create chimeras. We can come to see meaning and sense where there's just gibberish of our own making."

James felt deflated. "So you don't even want to look at the transcription?" he asked.

"Of course I'm as curious as you to know what the tablet says. But we must *know*, James; not engage in guesswork, however luminous. And, frankly, I want it to be your discovery when it does come; there's no need for me to have any more inscriptions to my name. I say come back – well, come back in a week and we'll see how your ideas have changed. Think about the variants. Think about other possibilities; go back to the images."

It felt like a dismissal. The Professor had no interest in reading James's transcription of the curse tablet that he himself had put in his way. It was the typical gatekeeping, James thought, of the elderly and credentialled scholar; "I covered my room in scraps of paper for weeks; I suffered, and so should you." But what if James was a more talented reader of Roman cursive than the Professor? What if he did represent a better quality of scholarship, a more insightful mind? They were inflated thoughts, and probably no good for him, but they offered some consolation in response to the Professor's rejection.

*

James had almost forgotten about his feeling of being followed, but that evening it returned with a new intensity. He found himself walking towards Wellington Square along St John Street, with the intention of cutting through Little Clarendon Street and onwards into Jericho. It was not yet late, but the nights were closing in now and the sodium street lamps were bright orange against a sky rapidly turning an intense midnight blue. High Georgian houses of smooth limestone reared up on either side of the street; there were lights in some of the windows, but every so often he had to step around a grille set into the street which concealed cellar windows and, usually, a pit of deep darkness. James found a childish fear arising in him; the child's fear of a monster reaching out from under the bed and grabbing one's ankles – but in James's case, it was connected somehow with these grilles, as if he expected something to reach up out of the blackness and coil itself around him.

He quickened his pace. The street seemed strangely empty; he would have expected someone around at this hour. As he gained the square, the high bushes in the middle of it loomed as silhouettes in front of the sky's fast-diminishing light; and as he glanced in their direction, it was as though something large disturbed the trees and began moving madly through the undergrowth. There were black metal railings between James and it – whatever *it* was – but this offered small comfort; and regardless of what anyone might think of him, James broke into a run, cutting down the path for bicycles and emerging at last into the lights of Jericho.

Work was out of the question. James was feeling increasingly unsettled by his own descent into a childish loop of fear and fear-confirmation. The feeling of being followed; the search for confirmation of the feeling; the feeling redoubled, and so on. He wondered if he would have felt different if the Professor had agreed to look at his transcription. As it was, he was cut off; the only person, in seventeen centuries, to have read that curse tablet – apart from the ill-fated Paul Foster, of course. As soon as someone else read it, it became the common property of scholarship; as things stood now, the exclusively personal connection between James and the words of the tablet was a source of mental unease.

He slept fitfully that night; once again, he was flea-sized, and dropped onto the vastly magnified surface of the *defixio*; and once again, he was fated to wander along the stylus-scratched paths of the letters. But this time it was different; dark, fluttering figures pursued him, gained on him, reached out horrible appendages in his direction; and all at once he found himself teetering at the edge of the giant tablet, over some vast abyss. And they were there with him, nudging, pushing him over the edge ... Each time the dream recurred during the course of the night, the fall into the void awoke him with a start, and the cycle began again. He longed for dawn.

*

The next day, James was reluctant to leave his room. He felt listless and unmotivated, and certainly unable to focus on work. Although he had no intention of going out, at about four o'clock he found himself in the street – he couldn't clearly recall how he had got there – walking west at speed. Just as earlier he had struggled to find the motivation to do anything, now he found himself unable to stop. It was as though a force separate from his will were moving his legs, as in the dream where he paced the grooves of the curse tablet. But James could be in no doubt he was awake; he was cold, and shivering, since he was only wearing a t-shirt. It was like running headlong down a hill, except there was no hill; he wanted to stop, but the pace was set, the trajectory could not be resisted.

He was not quite at a run, but he was walking at his fastest pace, with pain shooting up the back of his shins. He had turned onto the Oxford Canal now; that was when he began to feel, once again, that he wasn't alone. Something was moving along the canal path, keeping close to the bows of the narrowboats, loving the shadows, but matching his speed. Its movement was more of a glide than a walk, and

James could not bear to look at it; but the closer it drew to dusk, the more the thing seemed to gain on him by tiny increments. Where James had previously been walking in a straight line, he now began to veer wildly from side to side of the path – perhaps because his will was taking over now, and James himself wanted to continue moving away from the thing. But the effect was to bring him perilously close to the edge of the water, and when this happened the thing seemed to dart forward – as if eager to finish the deed by pushing James in. Panic took over then, and James forced himself into a run; this stabilised his course, and at the first opportunity he took a footpath and got away from the Canal. He ran the rest of the way back to his room, freezing and terrified. As soon as the door was shut and bolted, he reached for his phone, and found Alyssa's number.

They met at the Lamb and Flag; at least, James reasoned, there was no water for him to be drowned in between his room and the pub. Alyssa was late, but when she arrived she listened to his story with complete seriousness. She had her head in her hands by the time he finished.

"It's not as though you could have foreseen this …" she sighed.

"Yes, I know. You're welcome to your 'I told you so' moment. But I need your help, Alyssa. You're literally the only person I know who believes in magic, who takes this stuff seriously. And that includes me; I still can't believe this is happening for real. And maybe it isn't; maybe it is just inside my head. But either way I need to do something."

James had outlined the basic message of the curse tablet – although Alyssa made clear to him she had no desire to know exactly what it said: "If the curse falls on anyone who reads the tablet, that might include anyone who hears what it says as well," she warned him.

Alyssa pondered. "If we're talked about the logic of magic, then a magical curse can only be broken by magical means. Obviously we can't do anything to return to sender, because the sender has been dead for centuries. But there's always the option of destroying the curse itself."

"You're telling me to destroy a Roman artefact in the Ashmolean? How exactly am I supposed to do that?"

"Well, you're studying it – so if anyone has a right to ask to inspect it, it's surely you. It's not exactly the Elgin Marbles – it's a forgotten small find from an excavation in the eighties. But I'm not sure that's the answer anyway …" she stared into the middle distance. "The thing about written curses is that sometimes they *want* you to destroy the instrument of the curse. That just seals the curse on you. Destroy the curse, and you've closed off your options."

James clenched his fists. "Then what the hell do I do? Am I just doomed, like Paul Foster?"

"Maybe not. You told me the curse tablet was addressed to a god – no, I don't want to know which god it was. It's like a letter with a primary addressee; that's the god, not you. So what we could do is get the letter to the god."

"What the hell am I, some kind of divine postman?"

Alyssa shook her head. "You told me the tablet was discovered in a mere in Norfolk. If we can get it back there – back in the mere – then you might stand a chance. That would be repeating the original act; what started the magic going in the first place."

"I think you're completely bonkers, but I suppose it makes a mad kind of sense. Have you still got that car, Alyssa?"

She nodded. "All primed and ready to go."

"You mean you'd let me borrow it?"

Alyssa laughed. "Borrow it! Are you completely insane? You're being pursued by malevolent entities and you want to drive my car to Norfolk? They'd run you off the road in the first five minutes and the police would have to dredge my car from the Thames, with you in it. No thanks."

He buried his head in his hands. Alyssa reached out to touch one of them.

"No, James; you don't understand. I'm saying that *I'll* drive to Norfolk. They aren't after me, are they? I'm not cursed."

He looked at her through tears. "You'd do that for me? Seriously?"

"I don't really have much choice, do I? I can't let you die, James."

So it was settled. Alyssa would take the tablet back to Pucklemere, and by whatever means necessary, she would get it back into the water. James's challenge was to get hold of the tablet itself. Luckily, he vaguely knew the relevant curator at the Ashmolean; she had been there when he and the Professor first examined in the artefact. Accordingly, when Alyssa left to go he fired off an email to the curator, explaining he was struggling with interpretation of the tablet and begging to have one more opportunity to examine it in person the next day. And then he stayed at the bar while the pub filled up, until the bell rang for last orders and beyond, nursing a single half pint of lager that the landlord finally prised from his grasp. "You need to go home, mate."

James had a terror of leaving the warmth and light of the Lamb and Flag. Although he had barely drunk anything, he felt disoriented in the street. Clearly it had been raining, as the pavement was shiny with water. Stone faces of lions protruding from the wall next to him seemed to contort into awful grimaces as he shoved his hands deep into his pockets and began towards home. He was not sure how he made it back, or what was real or and what dreamt afterwards; a bush that seemed to lunge towards him from someone's front garden; black tentacles of darkness that seemed to lash out from a grating in the street, a drain bubbling as if disturbed by the writhing of some unclean aquatic creature – and always, the steady rhythm of one following, barely glimpsed out of the corner of his eye.

Somehow, James made it to the morning; and he noticed with relief that the curator had got back to him, promising to let him inspect the curse tablet later that day. He put on his best face for the visit to the Ashmolean, trying to hide the signs of sleeplessness and fear, and prayed that Siobhan, the curator, would leave him alone with the artefact.

"I know what box it's in; I've got the reference," he remarked lightly, as she opened the door that led downstairs to storage.

Luckily, she was having a busy day.

"Oh, OK then! I'll let you get it out yourself, then."

A moment later, and the accursed thing was in James's hands; not that he had any desire to look at it, but he needed to make a pretence of study. Ten minutes later, Siobhan came down to check how he was getting on.

"I'm nearly done, Siobhan, so I'll just put it back in the box when I'm finished." He said it with all the nonchalance he could muster. This was the crucial moment. If she insisted on returning it to the box herself, there was no hope of him absconding with it. There was a short pause as Siobhan considered her response.

"Could you, James? I've got a mountain of stuff to do."

His triumph was complete – for now. James slipped the curse into a pocket and carefully closed the empty box, restoring it to its former shelf. Since he had not asked Siobhan for the item's accession number, he hoped earnestly that she was unsure – or at least vague – on exactly which item he had been checking in the first place. That way it might be a long time before anyone noticed the item had gone missing. Perhaps he might even finish his PhD before the loss was remarked.

He hurried out of the Ashmolean; it was raining hard now. Sheltering under the architrave he texted Alyssa.

"I've got it."

A few minutes later her battered green Kia pulled up, and James passed the artefact through the passenger window. Alyssa wouldn't touch it. "Put it in this tub," she instructed.

"I owe you one, Alyssa."

She smiled wryly. "Well, it might not work. But I still think it's your best shot. Don't for God's sake go anywhere near the water."

And with that, she drove off. They had studied the route together in the pub last night, and James knew it would be at least three hours before she could throw the curse tablet back into the mere. Until then, he was alone with whatever Ventonaurus had set loose on him.

*

Three hours passed. Four. James had never fully understood, until that moment, what was really meant by 'an agony of expectation'. He tried to stay in his room. But sure enough, just like the night before, he found himself walking, as if pacing out once again the letters of the curse on the streets of Jericho. And then, before he knew it, he was standing on the high metal footbridge above Isis Lock. He had no clear memory of how he had got there, although his feet smarted.

The light was failing, the dark water swirled below him; and at either side of him, advancing towards him along the bridge, James became aware of two dark figures forming. As if assembled from the shadows themselves, they slipped out of the fabric of the bridge and became tall, gaunt yet faceless apparitions that began to lunge in his direction. Their intent was clear; James knew how this story ended. There was nowhere to run. But just as they were almost upon him, it was over. The figures were gone, their presence gone; and an old couple were walking a golden retriever along the Canal Path in the dusk.

The text from Alyssa came through just as James left the bridge.

"I did it. I put the curse back."

Abcester

Maureen had done everything she could to save St Michael's. There had been appeals – to the local community, to the diocese, to the nation. There had been interventions by prominent historians and archaeologists, letters to the newspaper, and of course a long correspondence with the conservation charities that Maureen hoped might take the redundant church on. There had been plans drawn up for a heritage centre, for a museum, for a community centre, even for a local shop with an integrated Post Office. But every time, neither the funding nor the will seemed to be there.

There was no changing the fact that Abcester was in the middle of nowhere. Important to the Romans, perhaps; but no-one came there now, not even on the way to anywhere else. And although St Michael's stood on an extraordinarily ancient site, and the church contained an interesting collection of Roman odds and ends excavated from the Roman town, the building itself was largely a Victorian replacement for earlier buildings; it failed to meet the charities' tests for architectural and historic significance. The Roman odds and ends – a couple of altars and some worn sculptures of forgotten gods – could, after all, be taken away to the county museum. And then the diocese would be free to sell the church, in the hope that some enterprising homeowner might buy a 'feature property' that was 'ripe for development'.

Maureen, the deanery's lay chair, had long since tired of the puns on Abcester as an abscess on the deanery; but the whole business had certainly made her life miserable for the last two years. At long last, the end came; the bishop came down for a final service, and a good portion of the village turned out – including some who, it seemed, were eager enough to hob-nob with the bishop but hadn't lifted a finger to help with Maureen's fundraising efforts.

"It's a shame no-one came up with any ideas for re-using the building," opined one of the visitors, a flashily-dressed retired GP, "No-one needs a church these days, but couldn't they have turned it into a Post Office or something?"

Maureen wearily explained, for the hundredth time, that it had all been tried. The bishop, who knew the grim facts as well as anyone, somehow forced an upbeat sermon that assured the congregation that they, and not a dead old building, were the real church, and that the church's closure was really a good thing because it was "releasing God's people into the community."

"What community …?" Maureen wondered, as she looked around at the grey heads of the great and the good of the parish, none of whom had managed to save the church – nor, in most cases, even tried. The vicar, an incumbent of twenty parishes – albeit soon to be nineteen – sat in her stall with a thousand-yard stare passing high over the heads of congregation.

There was one notable exception to the general indifference: Malcolm, the last remaining churchwarden, a quiet widower who had lived in the village all his life and knew it better than anyone.

"Well, I suppose I don't exist anymore," Malcolm remarked to her as they jostled at the coffee urn at the back of the north aisle. "As churchwarden, I mean ..."

"Our work isn't quite done yet, Malcolm. We need to take away anything moveable, remember."

"Don't you worry, I brought my trailer. When are those museum folks coming down to pick up the old altars and that?"

"I was on the phone to the museum just yesterday, but they can't give me a firm date yet; there are no conservators available, apparently, and they're waiting for some funding bid to go through."

"Give me a couple of strong lads and I'd get them in the trailer and up to the museum in no time."

Maureen laughed. "Well, you won't be getting me doing any heavy lifting. I only wish some of the young people did stick around ..."

She had inadvertently touched on a sore subject for Malcolm, whose sons lived respectively in London and New Zealand. Neither had been back to Abcester for years. But he carried cheerfully on, and when the last of the congregation had gone and the bishop hurried off to catch the train for an evening reception at the House of Lords, Maureen and Malcolm began the work of identifying what could be salvaged of centuries of worship. The rural dean insisted he *would* have stayed, but he needed to call urgently on a parishioner in hospital. Thus it was always with the rural dean, running somewhere else while asking Maureen if she could possibly shoulder yet another responsibility.

St Michael's had little to show for itself; years of neglect had rendered most of the moveable items unusable, or certainly undesirable. Maureen knew no church in the deanery would want the foxed King James lectern Bible or the huge Victorian Prayer Book, and such items were too common to fetch much on Ebay. The altar and pulpit frontals were crusted with mildew, and when she opened a drawer for vestments in the vestry Maureen found an apocalyptic mass of dead moths, expired in the midst of their feast on the church's ruined chasubles. On the other hand, there was still a set of hymn books and a heavy statue of St Michael spearing Satan in a colourful yet tasteful 1920s style.

And then there were the Roman relics. Maureen understood their historical importance, of course, but it was hard to say they were beautiful. When she and Malcolm lifted the statue of St Michael she noticed a particularly unpleasant one she had never seen before – presumably because the statue had hidden it. It was a squat altar that bore three grotesque faces and a legend in crude but still legible letters:

DIS
ANTVMNICOLIS
SACRVM

Maureen hoped that the very unpleasant aspect of the heads was down to weathering, which had obliterated some of their original features and given them the ghastly, half blank expressions they now wore. But she could not be certain. She remarked on the altar to Malcolm.

"Did you know about this one, Malcolm? I don't think I've ever seen it before."

"I knew about it."

His lack of elaboration suggested he had no desire to talk about the altar, but Maureen felt she had to press him to find out something.

"Do you know what it means?"

"We had some fancy Roman archaeologist come down a few years ago. Said the name on it was unique. Some gods of the underworld, he thought they were. God knows what unclean things they worshipped here. I never felt quite right about it, having them here in the church. But the vicar when I was a lad, Reverend Roper, he used to say the church was the only right place for them. And it was Mr Roper moved the statue to hide the devil stone."

"I'm sorry, 'the devil stone'?"

Malcolm laughed. "What we lads used to call it when we was choristers, back in the day. The vicar didn't like us calling it that, I can tell you."

Maureen looked again at the sculpture. Unique or not, she knew she disliked it intensely, and hoped the museum people would not be too long in coming to take it away.

*

Maureen hoped to find a good home for the massive statue of St Michael, but for the time being she kept him in her own hallway in Great Badeby, to offer a fearsome welcome to any visitors. One of those visitors was Malcolm, who called on her a couple of days after Abcester church's formal closure. His face was ashen when she opened the door.

"I'm sorry to bother you, Maureen, and I suppose it's neither your business nor mine anymore, but I had to tell someone."

Maureen ushered him into the house. "Of course you can tell me, Malcolm."

When she had settled him on the sofa with a cup of tea, Malcolm explained.

"There's been stuff going on up at the church; bloody sacrilege, that's what it is."

Maureen had heard the stories about how redundant churches sometimes attracted people intent on perpetrating some sort of sacrilegious rites, usually to impress or scare their friends. It would be sad indeed if Abcester became such a target.

"That's awful. We should report it to the diocesan office; the church is their responsibility now, at least until it's sold. Was there much damage?"

Malcolm took a sip of his tea. "Well that's the odd thing. You know I live almost opposite the church, in Old Bull Cottage? I saw lights in the church last night, right in the middle of the night. I called the police station, but they put me on hold so I gave up on that. I didn't think it was serious enough for me to call 999, and I wasn't going out there to get bludgeoned in the churchyard, so I thought I'd better wait till the morning and see the damage."

"And did you? What sort of damage did they do?"

"That's the odd part. There was no sign anybody had broken in. I still have my key; the rural dean said I could keep it for now, just in case. The place was all locked up as normal; there weren't any broken windows or whatnot. But when I got inside there was an odd smell, like something had been burning. And would you believe it, that damned altar had been pulled right out into the sanctuary, and there was a bit of burning on the top of it like someone had been using it as an ashtray. And there were flowers, too; someone had scattered a load of petals in front of it."

"Well, I must say I'm glad it wasn't worse."

"Worse?" Malcolm looked up from his tea. "I'm not sure how it could be worse, Maureen! That there church has been there for nigh on a thousand years, and probably more; whatever nasty things those Romans did there, we've kept a lid on them. And that bloody bishop just went and lifted that lid, and I think we're going to see what's under it. The sooner all those unholy things are gone, the better."

Maureen laughed. "Now come on, Malcolm, it's probably just someone messing around. Abcester's Romans are all dead and buried." She reassured him.

"It's the dead and buried ones I worry about," Malcolm retorted morosely.

Maureen felt that reassurance was the best thing she could offer, although she shared Malcolm's concern about people messing about in the church, and she promised to raise it with the diocesan office.

As it happened, she did not have long to wait. Shortly after Malcolm left, the diocesan office rang her. It was the Assistant Diocesan Secretary, explaining that she hadn't been able to get through to the vicar or the rural dean and pleading with Maureen to meet with a curator from the county museum, who had come to assess what needed to be done to transport the Roman remains.

Maureen texted Malcolm.

> Good news! Someone's come from the museum already. Not taking them away today but taking a look. I don't have a key though, so is there any chance you can meet us at the church at 3? Thx, Maureen.

*

Katie, the curator from the museum, was a lot younger than Maureen expected – or perhaps it was just that museum curators, like everyone else, seemed to be getting younger as Maureen aged. Dressed in a pink puffer jacket, the same colour as her hair, Katie was balancing on her heels with her hands in her pockets as Maureen strode up to the church porch. It was a damp October day, overcast and teetering on the verge of rain.

"You must be Katie, from the museum? I asked a gentleman to meet us here with the key; he used to be churchwarden."

Maureen explained who she was, and that she didn't actually live in Abcester, but realised she was chattering at the curator with increasing nervousness as Malcolm showed no sign of turning up. She glanced repeatedly at her phone, but there was no response to her message.

"I'm so sorry," Maureen apologised. "He normally gets back quite quickly, and he only lives across the street; I'll just nip over and see if he's home."

Leaving Katie standing there, Maureen hurried over to Old Bull Cottage and gave a sharp rap with the wrought-iron knocker, but there was no answer.

"I'm so awfully sorry you've come all this way, and now I can't let you into the church!" Maureen explained, as she returned to the curator.

"It's no trouble at all; I don't mind waiting. Or would you mind if I took a look at the outside of the church, and the rest of the site?"

Maureen was grateful for the response. "Oh, there's not much to see. I'm afraid there's nothing standing of the Roman town."

"I'm very interested in the Roman town, actually," Katie replied. "I wrote my Masters on Britain's smaller Roman towns."

Maureen laughed, as they walked together to the east end of the churchyard. "Well, Abcester is certainly one of the smaller ones! I mean, it's even smaller now – just a hamlet, really – but I can show you the ramparts."

They strolled over to a gentle rise at the edge of the churchyard; standing on top of it, it was possible to see that it was one part of a ridge that ran around most of the village, in the rough shape of a diamond – though cut into, of course by the four roads that came into the enclosure. To call it a 'rampart' was something of an overstatement, but Katie explained that it was clear evidence of rubble from a now-demolished Roman wall.

"It will be late, fourth century, from the time when even small places like Abcester started walling themselves in. It wasn't safe to be without walls anymore."

Katie went on to explain her interest in Abcester in particular; there had been no excavations there, she said, since the 1920s, when a pilot took an extraordinary aerial photograph of parchmarks and stimulated the first investigation.

"So that was when the altars were dug up, and put in the church?"

"The vicar was one of the people leading the excavation, I believe; so yes, the altars were dug up in this field here, to the south of the church." She gestured to the paddock, much beloved of dogwalkers. "It's a shame, really – there's so much we could do now, with modern methods; but at the time they didn't establish much about the context of the finds, and the County Archaeological Unit just doesn't have the funding. All they do is rescue archaeology now, if someone wants to build houses, or a road."

"Houses!" Maureen exclaimed, "Well, we'd be lucky to get any of those here. Abcester really is in the middle of nowhere. Most people move away."

She was interrupted by a phone vibrating in her coat pocket. It was Malcolm, of course.

"You can come over to the church now."

Smarting at the absence of any apology from Malcolm for his lateness, Maureen walked briskly back to St Michael's to find that the churchwarden had already let himself in. It swiftly became clear he had taken the opportunity to remove all evidence of the 'sacrilege' of the night before; apart from a faint smell of burning that Maureen thought she caught in her nostrils, there was no remaining sign of anything untoward, and the 'devil stone' had been pushed back to its previous position. But she should be grateful to Malcolm, she reflected, for putting things in order so she could show the curator the community cared properly for its Roman antiquities.

"It'll be a shame to lose them for the village, of course – they're a part of who we are; but the funding to turn the church into a heritage centre never came through, and they're much safer at the museum, aren't they?"

Katie took out her phone and began photographing the remains. "I'm just making sure we've got everything we expected," she explained. "What do you think one of these weighs?" she asked Malcolm, touching one of the altars to Jupiter Optimus Maximus.

"Five hundred pounds, easy," the old man replied. Katie looked at him blankly, but Maureen did the sum in her head.

"He means about two-hundred and thirty kilograms. You'll need proper equipment, lifting gear and pallets, if that's what you're asking."

Katie nodded. "Sure, I understand."

The curator moved into the sanctuary, continuing to snap pictures.

"We should really be wearing hard hats, you know – that's what the vicar told me – so we are being a little bit naughty – "

The words died on Maureen's lips as she stepped up into the sanctuary. A change of atmosphere hit her – something that she could only afterwards described as a thick veil of evil, as if she had pushed through a curtain into the domain of something unutterably malevolent. It was a thing so opposed to life that she felt as though the breath were being crushed out of her. Katie seemed not to feel it; the young woman strode resolutely towards the altar that bore the three grotesque heads – the one that had been hidden behind the statue of St Michael.

"This is the one I really wanted to see," she said. "It's a very special one."

"Is it, indeed?" Maureen was struck by a very intense desire to get out of there. She fumbled for any excuse to leave the sanctuary. "If you don't mind, I'm just going to check if anything got left in the pulpit," she declared. There were indeed a couple of old Prayer Books still there on the shelf beneath the lectern, but that was hardly the point. Maureen noticed Malcolm was standing well back from the sanctuary area. Perhaps he had felt the same thing she had. Katie, however, was enthralled, and continued to explain the altar even as Maureen felt relief wash over her, back in the nave.

"It's a unique inscription, 'sacred to the gods of Antumnos', which is a Gaulish word for the underworld. Maybe where the Welsh word for the underworld and for fairyland comes from, *Annwn*. And the three heads are pretty typical of Romano-British religion; there are often three of everything. But we don't really know anything about these gods, or who they were."

"Thank God for that," thought Maureen, without saying it; and she was relieved when Katie stepped back from the sanctuary. Or former sanctuary, whatever it should be called now. Malcolm hung back at the side-lines, his hands in his pockets.

"I think I've got all the information I need now." Katie said.

Maureen offered to walk her back to her car.

"It won't be too long, will it? The museum will take those things away?"

Katie looked puzzled. "Are you worried about security?"

"In a manner of speaking … yes, I suppose I am. I just wondered when you might be back to begin the process?"

"We're just waiting on some funding, so it might be a few weeks."

"Weeks!"

Maureen's tone must have alerted Katie to more than usual concern on her part. "I can tell you're worried about something. Is there a problem with vandals?"

That wasn't quite it, of course, but to Maureen it seemed as good a story to run with as any.

"Yes, there have already been some worrying signs. I just don't want the church to turn into a magnet for … you know …"

"Satanists? Yes, it is a bit of a problem for redundant churches. But you're better set up than most; you've got someone right on the doorstep, watching the place."

Katie left with an assurance to Maureen she would do everything she could to try to speed up the removal of the Roman artefacts; but it was small comfort. Rather than going back into that accursed place and speaking to Malcolm, Maureen drove straight back home.

*

The next morning Maureen almost expected a text from Malcolm, detailing further outrages in the night, and was relieved when her phone stayed silent. It was only when she ventured into the garden, late in the morning, that she realised something was awry. From the end of her garden in Great Badeby she could just about see the top of the squat spire of Abcester church, but as she reached the rose bushes a gust of wind brought the most horrible stench – and from Abcester's direction. It was not exactly like anything she had ever smelt before; living in a rural area, she was no stranger to pungent country smells like sileage, manure and slurry, but this was something else. It was a smell of death. And Maureen had no particular desire to get any closer. She went back inside and shut the French doors tight.

At lunchtime Maureen turned on the local radio station and found that the smell emanating from Abcester was already provoking interest.

> Residents of Abcester and Great Badeby have been reporting a very unpleasant smell across the whole area, which local people believe may be connected to a large sinkhole which opened up during the night in a field south of Abcester church. Environmental Health officials are reportedly on the scene, but refused to comment on what might be causing the stench. Officials believe no toxic chemicals are involved but are advising residents to keep their doors and windows shut.

Maureen decided to text Malcolm. There was no doubt he would have opinions of what was going on at Abcester.

"What's up with the big stink at Abcester?" she asked him.

"You should come down here. Bring a strong stomach." Was the response she received.

Maureen had no desire to venture into the stink, but she had called on Malcolm's good will a great deal over the last two years, and it seemed unfair not to drive over.

*

Abcester was only half a mile away, but as the car drew closer the stench began to seep into it, even with all of the windows and the ventilation closed. Maureen had soaked a handkerchief in perfume before she left, as some sort of protection against the worst of it, but she was unprepared for the wall of foulness that hit her when she opened the car's door outside Malcolm's cottage. She found herself holding her breath as she ran down the short path to his door, but on this occasion Malcolm was looking out for her, and quickly let her in.

"My God, what *is* that, Malcolm? I could barely breathe."

The smell was none too pleasant inside the cottage either, but at least it was no worse than inside the car.

"Unnatural, is what it is," Malcolm declared. "We've got to do something about this, Maureen. There's no *sinkholes* round here!" he spat out the word with contempt. "I lived here all my life, my father and grandfather afore me; and we never heard tell of any sinkhole. No, this – this is devilry, that's what this is!"

Devilry. It was a word from a play, an old-fashioned word conjuring images of sour-faced Puritans or burning witches. But with the seriousness that Malcolm said it, there in his unlit kitchen, it carried a weight that perhaps no other description could have borne.

"I know who's done this, Maureen. It's that bloody bishop, what with his de-consecrating …"

"The church hasn't actually been deconsecrated, Malcolm – "

"As near as damn it, it has! You take away God's worship, and there's other worships will take its place, and we've emptied that church of everything that's holy and left only what's unholy. I don't know why we're surprised about it, truth be told."

"But on the radio they had the Environmental Health people saying it was nothing dangerous …" Maureen feebly interjected.

"They said it was nothing *chemical*, not nothing dangerous. I've been up there myself; it's a ruddy great hole, five feet wide in the grass, belching God knows what. It's death, is what it is. Their place."

"Oh Malcolm, I haven't believed hell was actually under the earth since I was in ankle socks in Sunday School!" Maureen exclaimed. "Don't you think it's time you pulled yourself together and thought about this a bit more rationally? There are all sorts of weird and wonderful things in nature."

"This ain't a bloody David Attenborough documentary, Maureen," the old man snapped back. "This ain't nothing of flesh and blood we're dealing with. And I've an idea how we stop it."

"If you think the vicar or the rural dean will be interested, you might need to think again," Maureen scoffed.

"I don't need no vicar. What I need is that statue back."

"The St Michael statue? But we cleared the church, Malcolm; we can't go putting things back in it when the diocese is trying to sell the building."

Malcolm lowered his voice, speaking slowly and with conviction. "I don't care what the rules are, Maureen. I think that there statue was there for a reason. Do you remember, it was right in front of that evil old altar? And as soon as we moved it, things started happening."

Maureen had to concede that had been the order of events.

"And I know you felt it too," he continued, "when you were back in the church. It didn't feel right anywhere near that thing. I'd take a hammer to the damn thing if I wouldn't get arrested for criminal damage. But the next best thing we can do is put back that statue – at least until those museum people come back. I reckon it'll be safe there. It's because it's here, here where they were worshipped, that we've got problems. I reckon even evil things have got no power in museums, gawped at in glass cases."

Maureen could not but agree that bringing back the St Michael statue was preferable to Malcolm taking a hammer to an ancient monument and ending up in the Magistrates' Court. And he was right; she had felt it, even if she took no pleasure in acknowledging the fact.

"It doesn't feel quite real, does it?" Maureen reflected as she gazed out of Malcolm's kitchen window. "Like something outside of real life. But you're right, of course. I did feel something … awful, there in the church. Just in the sanctuary, close to that altar. I've never given any credence to all that claptrap about auras, and atmospheres, and spirits, and ghosts – and I still don't, I can tell you. But there's something amiss in that church all right."

"So, can I have your statue?"

Something about the situation seemed suddenly absurd, and they both burst out laughing; but Maureen soon turned to the practical aspect of the situation.

"We'll bring it back tonight; I know everyone's hiding from the smell but we don't want to arouse any suspicions or raise any questions by letting people see us carry St Michael back into the church."

"At night? You're bloody mad, woman."

Maureen laughed again. "I know, I know – but I think it has to be."

"I say we do it in the early hours," Malcolm said. "Are you up for an early start? I'd rather feel we had the dawn ahead of us than the night."

It made sense, and Maureen shared Malcolm's preference of having the hope of dawn; so they agreed to meet at half past six the next morning, about an hour before sunrise.

*

Maureen was late; she had a good deal of trouble lifting the statue into the back seat of the car on her own; last time, after all, she had had Malcolm's help. It was about four feet tall and carved from a single piece of wood. She could already smell Abcester, wafting its uncleanness across the fields. 'The Abcester abscess' she had heard the sinkhole called most recently on the radio, by local residents explaining they were staying with friends outside the parish until the source of the stink had been found out and dealt with. They just might be in luck, thought Maureen, as she slammed the car door on St Michael plunging his spear into a grim-featured devil.

Malcolm was at the church when she arrived, holding a flashlight by the open door. Between them they manhandled St Michael into the dark nave, trying to breathe through their mouths to avoid retching at the stink. Resting the figure on a pew, Malcolm reached out for the light switch.

"They've only gone and cut off the electricity!" He whispered loudly. "Or it's them; they prefer the darkness."

Maureen shivered, in spite of the exertions of lifting the heavy statue. "Malcolm, perhaps we should do this another time; I'm not sure I can bear to go into that sanctuary in the dark."

"And I've no doubt that's what they're counting on," Malcolm said. "They've laid claim to this place, but there's life in the old church yet. What we have to do is put that statue back, exactly where we found it. Whatever happens, whatever you see – just keep focussed on that."

Once again, Maureen had to concede Malcolm was right. Of course delay was unthinkable. They had to press forward. Luckily, Malcolm had a head strap for his flashlight and he proceeded to fix it to his forehead, blinding Maureen when he turned it towards her.

"Mind out, Malcolm! I can't see if you look straight at me."

Fortunately, they both knew the geography of the church well. It was not entirely dark; a dull blue light was beginning to gather at the bases of the windows, and Maureen was grateful that most of them were plain glass rather than the heavy stained glass of the Victorians. The figure of the crucified Christ in the east window was a shapeless mass, roughly kite-shaped, and not yet fully visible. But slivers of pre-dawn light caught the sheen of some of the pew edges. It was their feet that were in utter darkness.

The bearers of St Michael were approaching the steps of the sanctuary. This was the hard part. The darkness of the chancel radiated menace; something like the feeling of standing before the barred gates of a hostile embassy, guarded by armed, faceless soldiers. Not just a 'No Entry' sign, but a warning not even to dare have thoughts of entering.

"Pray, Maureen!" Malcolm hissed as he trod on the first step.

Maureen remembered a prayer she had loved so much as a child – not so often heard in church these days, but it always made her feel as though God was wrapping her in a warm blanket. It seemed the right one for that moment.

"Lighten our darkness we beseech Thee, o Lord, and by Thy great goodness defend us from all perils and dangers of this night; for the love of Thine only Son, our Saviour Jesus Christ …"

As she spoke the words softly beneath her breath, Maureen caught sight of what she thought was movement; and as her feet gained the sanctuary – "What sanctuary?", she thought bitterly – she was plunged once again into that well of evil where her strength had failed her before. She stumbled, and the weight of the statue seemed suddenly to become immense. The fluttering she saw out of the corners of her eyes in the semi-darkness began now to solidify into what she thought were three slightly luminous faces, placed at the north, south and east sides of the sanctuary. She knew she must not look at them. But she also knew what they were: huge, disembodied versions of those three hideous heads on the accursed altar. She was paralysed on the spot: unable to lift the statue, unable to drop it, unable to look; unable to close her eyes – while their malice pressed in on her from every side.

"Maureen!" Malcolm broke the silence – the pact of whispering – by shouting her name. It was a momentary intrusion of normality into a nightmare. "Heave!" he yelled.

And the statue fell into position.

Like a bath emptying fast when the plug is pulled out, Maureen felt the malevolence recede. As if it was withdrawing, somehow, into that stone that was now hidden before the form of St Michael. Malcolm let out a great groan of relief.

"Thank God! It's done. And thank you, Maureen."

Maureen could scarcely believe she was smiling, after experiencing all that. A nervous reaction, no doubt. Malcolm took off the flashlight from his head; there was now enough light to see the outlines of the familiar furniture of the sanctuary; an orange glow was appearing at the base of the east window, and above it the figure of the crucified took shape in the dawn light. It was at that moment that Maureen remembered those two old prayer books left in the pulpit.

"I say that that miserable business with the bishop wasn't the last service in St Michael's," she said, as she handed Malcolm one of the books, and turned the thin yellowing pages until she alighted upon the words of Morning Prayer. Sitting in opposite stalls, they read the old words as the sun rose on the village.

*

The stink stopped that morning, and a local farmer eventually filled in the 'Abcester abscess' with gravel. The people from the museum turned up with a van two weeks later, and all of the Roman antiquities were taken to the county museum, to be gazed at by bored schoolchildren learning about the Romans. The church was sold eventually; the retired GP bought it and turned into a big open-plan house with attractive mezzanine flooring. Maureen took back the statue of St Michael. It stands in her hallway still.

Nighthawk

"I don't think you heard me, Gerry," Vladko almost spat the words down the phone, "I told you clearly enough, you need to destroy it."

Gerry protested. "I don't see why I can't bury it somewhere. What difference does it make?"

Vladko's reply was slow and menacing. "Because, Gerry, if you bury it, someone might find it. And if someone finds it, they'll trace it back to us – " he raised his voice, "because some dead man – and I swear to God he is a dead man – put a photo of that thing on the web."

"C'mon, Vladko; you know it wasn't me. We've been over this …" he tried to hold back the fear in his voice.

"Maybe it wasn't you. But I swear to God, if you don't destroy it like I've told you to, I'll do the same to you as I'll do to whatever bastard put the photo online. And do I need to mention your daughter?"

Before Gerry could protest, the line went dead. Vladko had put the phone down. Gerry leant back against the concrete of the underpass, released a mingled sigh of repressed rage and relief, and lit a cigarette. It had been three days since the order came from the buyer to destroy the dish – once greatly desired, now unwanted. "Our buyers are special people," Vladko had explained, "they want a clean journey from the ground to their private collections. No leaks. If someone knows about the damn thing, their ownership is compromised; their privacy is compromised. These are serious collectors we're talking about here, Gerry …"

Vladko had arrived unannounced at Gerry's home with two 'friends', both alarmingly square-headed men of immense height, with unmerciful eyes – and demanded to see Gerry's phone. It was only after he had verified that Gerry had no images of the artefact that Vladko relented. He accepted it must have been one of the others.

Gerry understood the protocols: no photos. It wasn't rocket science; if the police came knocking he didn't want images of an illegally recovered artefact on his phone. He didn't need to be told twice. So whoever had put the image online was a complete idiot – and not because he had the police to fear. If Vladko and his friends didn't go after the culprit, the owner would; and whatever Vladko was capable of, he was a pussycat compared to some of the clients he worked for.

The image was already going viral on Twitter. Academics were debating whether the dish was a clever forgery or a hoax. It was only a matter of time before someone realised it might be a previously unrecorded and illegally recovered object. Of course, the news media weren't running anything yet without confirmation; that was some small mercy.

It made perfect sense that the buyer would want it destroyed. No doubt he or she had paid Vladko some proportion of the price to have it done away with, even if the sale was off; if Gerry was lucky, he might even see some of it. The provenance – or rather, the absence of a provenance – was tainted. People knew about the find. The pleasure of owning a treasure that no-one else knew about was what these deviants paid for, Gerry reflected; with laser-protected vaults under their mansions filled with secrets they delighted to withhold from the world, thumbing their noses at museums and archaeologists. It was a sick sport for them; the most absolute kind of ownership, because they owned the provenance as well as the artefact. No previous owners, no chain of possession, no auction houses, no meddling scholars. But they needed people like Gerry; metal detectorists with flexible ethics or, in Gerry's case, crippling gambling debts.

 He sauntered listlessly back to the house. Somewhere a dog was barking, and a streetlamp above him flickered with migrainous intensity. Ellie, to his surprise, was awake. She ran to him in her pyjamas as soon as the front door was open.

 "I was worried about you, dad! I thought those horrible men had come back."

 "I told you, they're not coming back. I just had some calls to make, that's all. Now, you should be in bed."

 She grinned, and he gave in. "Alright, you can have a quick snack. But nothing too sugary, mind."

 "Dad, I'm not six." She began ransacking the kitchen cupboards, looking for something to eat. Gerry crumpled into a chair and began to contemplate the work ahead of him. He had to find a way to destroy a priceless fourth-century silver dish; perhaps the finest example seen in Britain since the Mildenhall Treasure. And he would never be able to talk about it, not to anyone.

*

Gerry had been detecting in Wightmans Wood since he was a teenager. Everyone local knew it had something to do with the Romans; if you looked at the ground carefully you could see broken bits of tile and tesserae beneath your feet in the leaf litter. The old Ordnance Survey maps marked it as a Roman villa, and some Victorian vicar wrote a pamphlet about tracing a plan of walls in the wood, but it all seemed a bit speculative. No-one had done any work since; Wightmans was private land, even if locals went there all the time, and the owners certainly had no interest in archaeology. Detectorists had been caught there before and prosecuted for trespass, but Gerry was careful. Since he'd got into the game seriously, he'd started working at night. Night-vision had cost a fortune but it was worth it, and his investment soon paid off.

The finds had been small at first, but a decent source of income – things like keys, enamelled brooches, weights, base coins, the occasional denarius … but his first big find had been a beautiful crouching silver leopard. Cleaning it up took forever, and he could scarcely believe his eyes when it stood there, gleaming in front of him on the kitchen table. He kept it hidden from Ellie, though. It put him in a tight spot; you could sell small finds online, no problem; loads of detectorists did it. But Gerry knew the leopard was treasure trove; there was no way he'd get anything for it if he reported an item recovered illegally from private land. And that was how, eventually, he made contact with Vladko. The name came up in a conversation in the pub with some fellow detectorists – spoken of darkly, as someone you didn't really want to know. But he was out there, a presence and an option; and, most importantly, he was in touch with buyers.

Vladko was friendly enough at first. He wanted to know all about Wightmans Wood, "a new hotspot," as he called it. And it wasn't long before Vladko wormed out of Gerry the reason he was so keen to sell. Vladko had a gift for sniffing out people's vulnerabilities, and he soon recognised Gerry as a single father with a gambling problem, ripe for exploitation. Gerry got a decent price for the leopard, which was spirited away to the Emirates or somewhere, but then the pressure was on him to find more. Vladko's phone calls got more frequent, and more threatening.

"Are you going out tonight, Gerry? You're our man on the ground here. We need you taking this seriously. There are buyers waiting on this. Do you think that leopard could have been one of a pair? Are we talking a proper treasure here?" The questions came thick and fast.

A few decent coins turned up. More than a few, in fact. But Gerry knew there was no guarantee he'd get anything more out of Wightmans Wood. A few times Vladko or one of his 'friends' picked Gerry up in the night, driving him and a couple of other guys to some site – usually a place archaeologists were digging up before they built houses there, where Gerry and the others would break in with bolt-cutters and make a quick sweep. They didn't find much. All eyes were still on Wightmans Wood, and Vladko started sending other guys to help with the search. Gerry wasn't happy with that at all; the others didn't know the area; they weren't careful, as he was, and a whole crowd of them were bound to attract more attention. One of the idiots even brought a high-powered torch, and only one of them had night-vision gear like Gerry's. It was a recipe for disaster.

But then one night – he remembered it because it was Ellie's birthday – he got the dish. It was a terrific signal, and he was on his own that night, because it was raining and the others wouldn't come out. He had the devil's own job disentangling the mass of corroded metal from the root system of a tree stump, but pushing away the mud he was sure he was looking at a mass of silver sulfide and copper oxide coating what had to be a silver or silver-alloy artefact – although exactly what it was, at that stage, was still unclear.

When he was a safe distance away he immediately rang Vladko.

"I've got something, Vladko. It's big, and it's silver. Some sort of bowl or dish I think."

Gerry explained that he would need help cleaning the thing, whatever it was; the faster they could clean it, the faster it could be offered for sale to the buyers Vladko already had lined up. But Gerry insisted he control the cleaning process; he had seen enough cowboy cleaning of silver by detectorists and, as he explained to Vladko, they couldn't afford to compromise the artefact's value. Vladko agreed, and told him to find a place to keep the artefact safe that night. The next night Gerry received directions to a lock-up where Vladko had assembled the requested cleaning materials. There were three other men there; one of them a thug of Vladko's, and the others dodgy detectorists Gerry vaguely knew. He struggled to remember their names, and if he was being honest he didn't want to know them anyway. Vladko had other business to attend to and left his thug in charge, but under Gerry's direction the three of them began carefully cleaning the piece under the intense glare of the strip-lighting.

As soon as the mud was off and the first of the corrosion lifted, Gerry recognised instantly what this was.

"Mildenhall …" the word came to his lips, as he remembered the stories about how a farmer found the treasure while ploughing, cleaned it up and hid it on his sideboard until a visitor recognised it for what it was.

The Wightmans Dish (as Gerry christened it) was nowhere near as big as the Great Dish of the Mildenhall Treasure, which Gerry had seen many times in the British Museum; but the decoration evoked the same idea of a troop of figures dancing around a central face – this time the goat-like head of a faun rather than bearded Oceanus, though. The depth of the relief was incredible; the work of a master silversmith, undoubtedly on the same level as whoever made the Mildenhall dish. The figures of nymphs, naiads, dryads and maenads – all female, Gerry noted – threw out their lithe and lifelike limbs as they piped, span around and cavorted in their centuries-long dance around the faintly smiling face of the Great God.

Vladko was back in a few hours. Gerry had never seen him so happy. The cleaning was by no means done yet, but there was enough to show Vladko the quality of the piece. Gerry tried to explain something of its significance, of its relationship to other silverwork from Roman Britain … but Vladko was interested in what the buyer thought.

"Get it cleaned as quick as possible so I can get it to my photography guy."

*

The dish was cleaned and went to Vladko's photographer – presumably some professional who moonlighted for Vladko's operation. A couple of days later Vladko called Gerry and told him he was coming round with the dish.

"It's safest with you, history man. You're the one who cares about the damn thing!"

And so it was that the Wightmans Dish returned to its initial hiding place in Gerry's garage, in the crawl-space for mending a car's chassis, which Gerry kept concealed under some old carpet.

"I want to move this on quickly," Vladko explained. "It won't be with you more than a few days. Keep your phone close."

That was when all hell broke loose because the picture of the dish surfaced online.

Ellie was happily eating cereal in her pyjamas while Gerry reflected on the point he was now at in his life: about to destroy one of the most important Roman artefacts excavated in Britain since the War, because some faceless foreign buyer wanted it gone before anyone had the chance to see it. He knew there was only one way to do it properly. The next morning, once Ellie had left for school, he went to the garage and lifted the dish out from its hiding place, wrapped in tea-towels. He brought it into the back garden; no-one could see him if he sat directly behind the garage, and the garden looked out over the fields; his was one of the last houses on the estate. For some reason, he preferred to do this in the open air. Gerry stared down at the pair of bolt-cutters at his feet. Unthinkingly, he was still cradling the dish as if it were precious. But it was worthless now. Worthless to everyone but him, that was.

Kneeling on the overgrown concrete, he set down the dish and began to unwrap it. And there it was, gleaming in front of him. The Bacchic dance was about to come to an end. As Gerry laid hold of the bolt-cutters he heard a faint buzzing; at first he thought it was some machinery he had left on, but it seemed to be in his ears themselves. High blood pressure, he thought. It was no wonder.

Slicing through the silver was no trouble, of course. The bolt-cutters were made to cut through steel. He began with a series of incisions all around the edge. Metal jaws sliced through the limbs of the dancers, momentarily flattening their ancient features before they buckled and snapped. The buzzing seemed to get louder. But there was a job to be done. What melancholy Gerry had felt at first turned to a cold indifference as the beauty and aesthetic unity of the dish was obliterated. One by one, he crushed and snipped away the dancers, until only the face of the goat-god remained. He was clearly imagining things, because the god's eyes seemed to follow his own, and what he had once thought was a faint smile – a smile of benevolence, even – seemed now more like a snarl. Perhaps not so skilled a piece after all, he reflected, as he finally split Pan from beard to horns. That was it. The dish was in pieces. Scrap bullion.

But Gerry knew enough to realise he could not stop here; each one of these fragments, even in a damaged condition, could still tell a story to an archaeologist. He scooped the pieces into a plastic carrier bag, and set off for Hugh's. He knew Hugh from the pub; Hugh's son went to Ellie's school, but there was one crucial fact about Hugh that made him useful in this situation, and that was his possession of a kiln. He had built it in his back garden years ago, fancying himself as a potter, and still fired the occasional rustic cup or plate. Gerry had held a long conversation with Hugh about it all – in part out of genuine interest, but mostly because a kiln was a useful thing to have access to if ever Gerry was ever in need of high temperatures to melt metal. Gerry also knew Hugh had a record; only a few youthful indiscretions, to be sure – but enough for Gerry to be reasonably confident he was not a man who would run to the police at the first sign of something potentially illegal.

Gerry was pleased to find Hugh at home.

"Gerry, mate!" He opened the door in the uniform of a local supermarket. "I just came off the early shift. What can I do you for?"

"There's fifty quid in it for you." Gerry gazed at Hugh carefully, gauging the man's reaction. He smiled, as if he thought Gerry were joking, then narrowed his eyes into a questioning expression.

"Fifty quid to do what?"

"Fifty quid to let me use your kiln."

"My kiln? For what? If you want to fire something you don't need to pay me, mate – and certainly not fifty quid!"

"Let me come inside, and I'll explain."

Hugh stood back from the door and Gerry entered, giving his carrier bag a deliberate clink as he did so.

"Hallmarks." He said, as Hugh closed the door behind him. "They're the bloody devil, they are. Raise all sorts of questions."

"Now listen, Gerry; if this stuff isn't above board I'm not doing anything that makes me an accessory."

"Accessory to what?" Gerry laughed. "I'm offering you fifty quid to let me melt down some hallmarked silver. There's nothing illegal about that. It's just scrap; but it's a lot easier to sell on as bullion without the hallmarks."

Hugh squirmed uncomfortably. "This doesn't seem right to me, Gerry. You know I've been in trouble with the law before, and Susan – she's made me promise I'll have nothing to do with anything that even seems suspicious."

"A hundred, then."

Gerry could feel Hugh's resistance giving way. "All right, then. Give it here." He reached out for the carrier bag.

"It's OK, Hugh. I do the melting. You just tell me how to get the thing going. It needs to get past eight hundred degrees. You can just toddle off and put the kettle on, or something."

"Eight hundred? That's not hot for a kiln. But you'll need some sort of crucible." Hugh dug out an old mortar from the kitchen. "I don't think Sue will miss this. This will have to do."

Hugh fired the kiln, and then Gerry waited until his host was back in the house before placing the ruined fragments of the dish in the mortar. With a stick he shoved it into the kiln and waited. The roar of the kiln was hollow, like the blowing of some vast breath through immense reed pipes; and for a moment, in his mind's eye, Gerry pictured the grinning face of the god as the dancing figures continued their movement around him, their feet scattering sparks before the whole procession dissolved in fire. He must have fallen into some sort of reverie, because Hugh tapped him on the shoulder.

"It'll be way hotter than eight hundred by now."

Gerry nodded. He agreed to come back for the silver once the kiln had cooled down. It didn't matter now, anyway; it was just a lump of metal. The only reason he needed it was to show it to Vladko.

*

The little silver hemisphere that Gerry extracted from the mortar and presented to Vladko that evening matched the weight of the Wightmans Dish. Vladko seemed satisfied that Gerry had indeed followed through on total destruction.

"It was Viktor, by the way." Vladko remarked.

"Viktor?"

"We found the photo on his phone. He's been … educated." Vladko and his 'friend' shared a humourless laugh. For Gerry, it was an unwelcome reminder of the violence of Vladko's business; violence that he did his best to try to avoid.

"It's a shame, the dish. A big waste," Vladko remarked. "But that's all the more reason for you to get back out there, detector boy." Vladko pummelled Gerry's shoulder affectionately. "Those treasures won't find themselves."

*

Gerry found himself oddly averse to the idea of going back to Wightmans Wood. He had never been afraid of the dark before; it was one reason why he was good at what he did. Darkness was just an obstacle, like roots or mud. But he found it difficult to shake the idea that someone, or something, was waiting for him there. It was a full moon; bright enough, perhaps, even to lay aside the night-vision. Bright enough for it to be rather foolish to go detecting at all. But the shortfall had to be made up; Vladko had let down a client, and it was the little people who had to pay. The sphere of the moon above the wood could have been that silver dish, gleaming forever in Gerry's conscience. But he tried to push away such thoughts as he retraced his steps to the dish's findspot.

The buzzing in his ears was not the detector; he hadn't even put his headphones on. It was the same buzzing he had heard when cutting up the dish, and it intensified as he approached the stump where he first laid eyes of that lump of mud and metal. No, not a buzz; more like a hum, and a hum sounding more and more as though a living voice produced it. Something caught at his clothing; a branch, presumably. But then the second time it was more clearly a grab. He wavered on his feet, casting his eyes wildly around him. He saw no-one; but an instant later a cold hand was in his, and Gerry was being dragged forward, unable to disengage as he became part of a wild, desperate dance around that tree stump.

The speed was incredible – his feet barely touched the ground as he was drawn in a great circle, twigs and thorns ripping his clothes and skin. The hum became a long, drawn-out note on a reed, and as he careered through the undergrowth Gerry began to see them for the first time; the slender, attenuated beings who drew him into their dance, and yet for all their apparent insubstantiality held him with an unyielding grip. His heart pounded; he was at their mercy. A second note sounded on the reed, and he was able to turn his head and glimpse the moonlight shining full upon the tree stump, the centre of their wild orbit, and the outline of a figure that was beyond animal or human. A terrible yell of praise went up from the maenads. And then the god turned his face.

The Shrubton Oracle

The news that David Lynsard, the eccentric billionaire, would be reconstructing the famous temple of Apollo at Shrubton came as a shock to the archaeological community. Projects like this, if they happened at all, took years to orchestrate, to fund, and to publicise. But within a few months of purchasing the estate, it became clear that the Australian entrepreneur was determined to restore to Shrubton, at full scale, what had put this otherwise rather obscure corner of the West Country on the map: the extraordinary octagonal temple whose remains first came to light in the 1970s. And Lynsard was prepared to spare no expense in doing so. The best experimental archaeologists from across Europe were drafted in for the project, and most agreed to participate – after all, stable work for an archaeologist (and no apparent upper limit on the salaries participants could ask for) was not to be sniffed at.

The original Shrubton temple had been, like many of the more monumental Roman religious buildings of western Britain, a latecomer; a fourth-century construction which, according to the lead archaeologist Judith Brant, was almost certainly built in the brief reign of the Emperor Julian when a 'pagan revival' swept through the prosperous estates of Britannia Prima – today's Cotswolds. There were hints of some sort of Iron Age worship on the site, but Iron Age archaeology was tricky at the best of times, not least when the

Romans stuck a great big building on top of it. But the pattern of revival of pre-Roman sacred sites was consistent with the period, when late Roman shrines often popped up on top of some half-remembered Iron Age sanctuary. Shrubton was sited in a river valley – today little more than a trickle, and the Romans' elaborate terracing was long gone. All that remained of the temple – or at least of the spoil-heaps of the earlier excavation – were some lumps and bumps in the close-cropped grass, home to a few white-faced Somerset sheep.

Rebuilding the temple would be one of the largest experimental archaeology projects ever attempted in Britain. The old excavation had been one of the most thorough of the period, and Judith was confident there was enough information to produce a plausible reconstruction; but the new temple could not, clearly, be built on the foundations of the old. Yet David was eager for it to be located as close as possible to the original site, and Judith and her team eventually alighted on a spot a few metres closer to the river that geophysical surveys revealed to be more or less barren of archaeology. Accordingly, work began on the temple platform, a brilliant white marble-faced rectangular structure rising fifteen feet in places in order to ensure a level foundation for the temple itself, with wide, sweeping steps at the western and northern ends. The empty west end of the platform was the forecourt of the temple, where once the congregation had gathered and sacrifices were offered on a glistening white altar.

The platform was an extraordinary achievement in and of itself, conveying instantly how monumental the Shrubton complex was. But it was just the start. From the east end of the platform the brick structure of the temple itself now began to rise: first the base of the plain brick cella, and then, around it, a magnificent octagonal colonnade-ambulatory of brick and mortar arches supported on elaborate columns of Purbeck marble. Within two years it was all finished, and Judith was able to lead the first delegation of leading Roman archaeologists on a private tour of the site. There was a degree of scepticism within the group; private money always provoked cynicism, and the preconceived idea that David Lynsard was 'disneyfying' Romano-British religion was at the forefront of some of the party's minds – Judith had gathered that much from the conversation at lunch. On the other hand, the world of Roman archaeology – and Roman experimental archaeology, in particular – is a small one, and so many people had worked on the project that most of the visiting dignitaries knew at least one person who had received a paycheque from David. To that extent, the project already had the establishment's seal of approval – many reputable archaeologists had taken the billionaire's shilling.

The effect of the completed temple in the landscape was magnificent. It was like stumbling upon Ravenna's basilica of San Vitale in the middle of a Somerset field, except raised on a platform that hinted at Colchester's Temple of Claudius, or even modern Rome's Altare della Patria. Although built primarily out of brick, the octagonal temple was richly ornamented with stonework and its roof bristled with extraordinary terracotta decorations; the closer the group drew to the building, the clearer it became that Lynsard had spared absolutely no expense whatsoever; each craftsperson, working at the top of their profession, had been allowed free rein to realise their fantasy of what the most lavish Roman decorative features could look like. The billionaire himself, dressed in a loose hemp shirt, was waiting in the shade of the colonnade-ambulatory and sauntered out to meet the archaeologists as they entered the temple forecourt. An empty socket marked where the main altar ought to be, but the open drains for catching the sacrificial blood followed the excavated originals exactly.

He held out a suntanned hand to proffer his characteristically firm handshakes. "Dave Lynsard," he said, needlessly introducing himself to everyone.

"I want to thank Judith here," he began, laying a hand on her shoulder, "for pulling this all together. It's just been incredible. And I hope you'll agree the result is truly remarkable."

The Australian strode quickly ahead of the group, gesturing this way and that at features he thought worthy of note – the acroterial terracotta Gorgons' heads on the gables, the late Corinthian-style capitals on the ambulatory columns, the different types of marble. Once they were inside the ambulatory itself it became clear that Lynsard had insisted on even greater attention to detail, with extraordinary paintings depicting the deeds of the god Apollo, in a variety of different Pompeian styles, covering most of the plastered walls within. Judith found it very funny that the god was always a younger version of Lynsard himself. Narcissism finds a way, she reflected.

"We had to get in fresco artists from Florence specially to do those," Lynsard casually explained, before ushering the group through high cast bronze doors into the cella itself. It was an empty, cool and surprisingly narrow space – rather like being at the base of a tower or a disused windmill, but greenish light poured in from above through large windows made of authentically manufactured Roman glass. At the very top a forest of beams held up the tiled roof. The first few metres of the inner walls of the cella were of translucent-seeming grey-white Carrara marble. In spite of Judith's centrality to the project it was her first time in the cella itself, which had only just been finished in the last few days; and indeed it was the first time she or anyone else in the group had ever felt what it was actually like to stand at the heart of a Romano-Celtic temple – not that anyone, other than the priests who tended the shrine, would ever have been permitted inside this holy of holies in a functional temple.

"Wow, this is one expensive folly!" Judith heard one of her colleagues whisper loudly as he left the cella.

"Can I ask, Mr Lynsard," a prominent curator interjected, "whether you have any plans to open the temple to the public? Do you have any educational aims in mind?"

Lynsard nodded. "Absolutely. I want people to see it; I want them to realise what people were capable of in Roman Britain. That it wasn't some backward province full of downtrodden Celts and brutal legionaries. A building like this is Roman, but it's also Celtic. The melding of two cultures, to the benefit of both."

"I notice there aren't yet replicas of the cult statue, or the altars," a leading academic observed.

"Oh, we'll be getting around to that," Lynsard replied. "And I'm hoping we can go one better than a replica of the statue. My lawyers tell me I can share with you that I'm in negotiations with the British Museum for a loan of the head of Apollo that was discovered in the excavations."

Judith was a little surprised that David chose to share the news quite so early on. The loan – accompanied by a substantial donation, of course – was contingent on Lynsard Enterprises developing the temple as a visitor attraction. They wouldn't loan the head to a private collector, in other words. And Judith knew that, while the temple seemed complete, they were some distance away from opening to the general public; the infrastructure simply wasn't in place yet.

*

Although no-one from the press was allowed to accompany the archaeologists and curators, Lynsard's own official photographer was present to record the event and the visit generated significant press attention – as well as much public clamour for access to this remarkable new visitor attraction. But the Australian had something in mind beyond the handsome wooden visitor centre that was going up on one side of the field. One day he summoned Judith to see him at Shrubton Hall. He received her in one of his sparsely furnished rooms; living a hermit-like life was part of his image.

"You know we've got people working on the altars now?" He motioned Judith towards an uncomfortable piece of furniture that approximated a chair. "Can I get you a smoothie?"

"No, thank you. Yes, I've seen some wonderful pictures of the progress on the main altar. Exquisite detail."

"And the BM's finally playing ball on that loan, so we should be getting our boy back!" Lynsard took a sip of his own unappetising health-shake.

"Yes, I've been copied in on the plans to display the head."

Lynsard stared for a moment into the middle distance, towards some gruesome-looking gym equipment in the corner of the room.

"There's something I wanted to run past you, though, Judith …"

She nodded. When it came to Dave Lynsard, Judith had long since learnt that for him to 'run something past' you meant he had already decided on it. "I've been talking to Ross, the sculptor, about taking the experimental archaeology a bit further. I want us to start thinking about the visitor experience; and I want the visitors to feel like they're seeing a working temple."

Judith shifted uncomfortably against the silicon ball pressing into her back. "I'm sorry, I don't think I quite understand you, David ... a working temple?"

"With priests, and worshippers, and libations ..." Lynsard laughed, "obviously the animal welfare people wouldn't let us do animal sacrifices! We need the sheep to keep the damn grass down anyway. Not to mention I'm a vegan ..."

Judith did her best to laugh along with the billionaire, but she struggled to decide if what he proposed was tacky or ghoulish. Perhaps both. Actors trying to re-create the past? Wasn't that what people's imaginations were for?

Lynsard continued. "I've been in touch with an agency. There's no end of young actors out there looking for a gig. But I want people with an interest in history – or archaeology, even better. I've got a list of names – some of them have even worked on digs."

Judith was not altogether surprised that there was some crossover between the ranks of out-of-work young actors and out-of-work young archaeologists; acting and archaeology were both professions that attracted idealists yet offered them little realistic prospect of future work. She dreaded to imagine what bunch of misfits Lynsard would assemble, and hoped the whole thing would come to nothing. But over the coming months the entrepreneur kept her updated; until one day, a little under a year later, she was invited to meet the troupe.

The official opening of the visitor centre and the site to the public was scheduled for July, but Lynsard insisted the actors familiarise themselves with their roles beforehand via an intensive summer camp – "very Method," Judith reflected, remembering some of her own contemporaries at university who had taken themselves much too seriously as Method actors and insisted on strutting about in costume for days. Accordingly, the actors lived at a campsite at the edge of the woods and were to spend their days either as priests, slaves or worshippers seeking healing or visions from the god.

When Judith first met them they were not yet in costume. The tallest, a young man named Carl with dark curly hair and a very Roman-looking beard, was selected as the principal priest of Apollo. A young woman named Gemma, who was to be a Romano-British peasant seeking healing for an eye complaint, seemed to be the most critical of the group. When Judith arrived at the visitor centre Gemma was boldly interrogating Lynsard on the project.

"What are your thoughts on the ethics of the performance?" She asked him.

The billionaire chuckled, seeming rather to enjoy being confronted without a trace of sycophancy.

"The ethics? The Romans have been dead for two thousand years, dearie."

"That's not what I mean. You're making a conscious decision to ask us to perform religious practice. Now, is this supposed to be entertainment? Because if we're presenting religious practice as entertainment – even if it's obsolete rituals – we're sending a message about respect for faith traditions. Would you expect to see actors imitating Hindu worship in a museum exhibit about India?"

Judith decided to throw in her own viewpoint. "In any heritage attraction there will always be an element of entertainment. But that doesn't mean that's what you're there for."

"Absolutely not," David added. "This place is about education; that's what I've always intended. Schools groups come free, and they get priority over other visitors. I want people to come here to learn about the Romans."

Gemma wouldn't let go. "You've described what we've been asked to do as experimental archaeology; but experimental archaeology means finding things out about the past by making or doing them. That suggests something beyond just performance."

Lynsard smiled. "Why do you think I've asked you to be here day and night for the next three weeks?"

"So, what are we supposed to be finding out …?" Carl, the designated priest of Apollo, asked.

"How Roman religion worked," Judith replied. "What were the mechanics of it? What happened if someone brought an offering for the priests – what did they do with it? How did a Roman ritual meal work? We have a lot of theory, but also a lot of questions."

"Wasn't there supposed to be an oracle here?" Carl asked. "Like the one at Delphi?"

It was a sore point for Judith. Part of her PhD had focussed on the possibility of an oracular cult at Shrubton. There were a couple of surviving inscriptions that referred to visions of the god, suggesting an incubation cult where worshippers slept in the precincts, waiting upon visions of the god; but a fragmentary Latin inscription, apparently reading FATVM ACCIPE ('accept your fate'), suggested to Judith something more – because it was apparently a translation of one of the so-called Delphic Maxims, associated with the famous Greek oracle. The question of the oracle was one on which her examiners had given Judith a hard time; after all, the idea of an unrecorded oracular shrine in Britain was far-fetched, to say the least. On the other hand, the fourth century was poorly attested anyway, and the presence of an oracle would go some way towards explaining why Shrubton was developed well beyond the scale of most Romano-British temples.

"We don't know." Judith answered Carl. "There may have been an oracle; it's a theory. But we just don't know."

"It's up to you to make the temple your own," Lynsard added. "I'm asking you to be faithful to the sources; to the reading list I've sent you. But beyond that, I want you to find your own rhythms, to find your own way of doing things that makes sense in the space; you're the ones writing the script."

"Improv on steroids," Carl remarked, raising a few laughs from the others.

They walked over to the temple. The first major difference Judith noticed was the installation of a magnificent marble altar, decorated with lifelike garlands and bucrania, with the inscription DEO APOLLINI SACRVM cut in deep, crisp letters. It was an exact reconstruction of the much-broken altar found in 1974 and now in pieces in the county museum, apart from the replacement of the original dedicator's name with Lynsard's: DAVIDVS LYNSARDVS DEDICAVIT. Judith winced at the alteration. Narcissism again.

In the temple cella there now stood a life-sized transparent figure of the god in two-dimensional acrylic, specially designed to hold the surviving head of the cult statue in the position it might once have occupied in a long-lost cult image. The effect was strange, as if the stone head were hovering, disembodied, a few feet from the floor, and was enhanced by spot lighting in the pavement that lit up Apollo's worn features and boyish curls – curls very much like Carl's, Judith thought. There were other additions, too; embroidered hangings on the walls depicting the lyre of Apollo and hanging bronze lamps and incense burners, which were already belching out an oracular cloud that partially hid the cult statue. It was all very atmospheric – a strange combined evocation of ancient and modern.

*

Judith had no formal role in overseeing the re-enactors – David was taking that in hand personally; and in any case she was a field archaeologist and temple specialist, not an experimental archaeologist. However, her new office was located on the first floor of the visitor centre and overlooked the temple, where she had a distant view of anything happening on the temple platform. The re-enactors soon settled into a pattern, and Judith frequently saw a little column of smoke ascending from the altar – presumably burning offerings of grain. Although Judith did not venture over to the temple – David had given instructions that the re-enactors were not to be disturbed – some of the re-enactors did sometimes find their way to the visitor centre. They quickly learnt Judith had a coffee machine in her office that she was willing to share; and the fact that Judith was the lead archaeologist rather than the site manager helped the young people feel she was not checking up on them. She became, instead, something of a listening ear.

One person who never came over to the visitor centre was Carl, the priest. Simon, one of his acolytes, came over initially but thereafter largely stayed at the temple. Gemma was particularly scathing of Carl.

"He's gone scarily full Method," she explained to Judith one afternoon over a cappuccino, sitting in the office in incongruous Romano-British tartan trousers. "It worries me a bit, honestly. Last night he told me I had to incubate."

"You mean sleep inside the temple?"

Gemma smiled. "Oh, he won't let any of us inside the temple now. The cella is off-limits except to him, Simon and Tim. But he told me I needed to spend the night in the temple colonnade. It was bloody cold, and of course I could only have the authentic coarse wool blankets."

"What was the point of that?" Judith asked.

"Oh, apparently the god is supposed to appear to me in a dream or something." She took a sip of the coffee.

"And did he?"

Gemma looked away for a moment, smiling nervously.

"No, of course not. I did have some pretty funny dreams, though."

"Oh, really?"

Gemma seemed surprised that Judith was showing genuine interest. "Yes; it was like I woke up, there in the colonnade; and the moon was very bright. And I looked over to the altar and there were figures gathered round it. Not Carl and the boys, but old men in white robes, with hoods pulled up over their heads. One of them had hold of a sheep by its horns and they were talking in Latin, I suppose. The one with the sheep kept looking at me and asking me something, like I was supposed to speak; and then another one of them pulled a knife from a fold in his robe and just sliced open the sheep's throat. There was so much blood! It was pouring out like a fountain, running into those gutters. And they turned towards the temple and started chanting. The big bronze doors were closed, but I had this strong feeling they were going to open, and that I was supposed to go in there. And I wasn't sure I wanted to see what was inside, still less go in.

But that was it – that was when I woke up, and I was lying on the cold flagstones and the sun was coming up behind the woods."

"So did you tell Carl about the dream?"

Gemma sighed. "He makes all of us tell him our dreams; it's one of the rules he's made."

Judith raised her eyebrows. "OK … And what did he say?"

Gemma turned to face the older woman. "That's when he got a bit scary. He said he thought the figures at the altar were expecting me to speak. That they thought I was the oracle. And now he keeps going on about me becoming the voice of the god. He doesn't seem able to break out of character. It's getting creepy, to be honest."

Judith shook her head. "I don't much like the sound of this, Gemma. It sounds like Carl's getting a bit controlling. The whole priest of Apollo thing has gone to his head. Be honest with me: do you want to stay, or do you want out? I'll smooth things over with Mr Lynsard if you want to leave."

Gemma stood up. "There's only a week to go. I'm fine, really. I can give Carl as good as I get. And I need the money, if I'm honest."

So Gemma went back to the temple, but Judith was left with a feeling of unease. She was unsure what to do; whether to tell David about this, or see how things played out. She chose the latter course.

*

It all happened a few days before the experiment was due to draw to a close. The first visitors – a local primary school – were expected in less than a week. Martha, another of the re-enactors, came running into Judith's office.

"It's Carl!" She shouted. "He's gone crazy and shut Gemma in the temple!"

The re-enactors were not allowed phones – it was one of Lynsard's stipulations – so Judith grabbed hers from her desk in case she needed to call the owner, or even perhaps the police. Carl's behaviour had certainly sounded 'off' from Gemma's description of it – she had heard of actors tipped over the edge by immersive performance, and that might be happening here.

"Now, what the hell is going on?" Judith demanded as she reached the platform, only to find most of the young people gathered in a knot around the temple's bronze doors. Carl, in his white robes, leant heavily against the doors to hold them shut while other members of the group tried to physically pull him away; even Simon and Tim, who played the roles of his priestly assistants, were remonstrating with him. But Carl's face was entirely calm, and he was a big man; the others seemed wholly ineffective in moving him an inch. And then, above the hubbub, Judith heard it; the bronze doors virtually sound-proofed the cella, but rising up through the windows at the top of the building she heard Gemma's scream – not short, panting screams of panic but a protracted, tortured howl of a kind Judith hoped never to hear again.

She was now standing directly behind Carl.

"Stand back from the doors! The play's over. If you don't move right now, I'm calling the police." She held up her phone.

Carl, to her surprise, shrugged and stepped back.

"It doesn't matter now, anyway." He said. "She wasn't strong enough."

The doors were immensely heavy, and Judith needed the help of three people to haul them open. At first, the cella seemed empty – until Judith caught sight of a pile of green and grey woollen clothes in front of the image of the god. It was Gemma. Judith called an ambulance, of course. But it was too late.

*

The reconstructed temple at Shrubton never did open to the public. For David Lynsard, the tragic death of one of his re-enactors was an embarrassment. Local interest in the temple project meant it was a major story in the local and even the national press. Gemma's parents wanted a charge of manslaughter against Carl, but he went to prison for a few weeks on a conviction for false imprisonment instead; there was insufficient evidence, the defence argued, that Carl could possibly have known that Gemma would suffer a panic attack, or that such an attack could lead to her death. Lynsard held on to the Shrubton estate but went back to Australia; he hardly needed the money from visitors to his temple, after all. The head of Apollo went back to the British Museum, and Judith found herself redundant. It was hardly a good position to be in when approaching fifty; but it was worth it, Judith considered, if she never had to go anywhere near that temple again.

ALSO PUBLISHED BY ST JURMIN PRESS

F. K. Young, *Yellow Glass and Other Ghost Stories*

The stained glass of a French cathedral is cursed by dark magic; an Icelandic rune raises a terrifying revenant; a fossil triggers an incursion from the fairy otherworld; three men are mysteriously burnt to death in an open field; a mysterious book haunts the dreams of three people over decades. Featuring seven stories of the supernatural and macabre, including 'This Is My Book' (winner of a prize in the 2018 'Ghosts in the Bookshop' short story competition), historian F. K. Young's début collection of ghost stories explores the terrors that await incautious delvers into the unquiet past…

ISBN 9780992640484
125pp.
Available from lulu.com

M. H. James (ed. Francis Young), *Bogie Tales of East Anglia*

Originally published in 1891, *Bogie Tales of East Anglia* by Margaret Helen James was the first book devoted to the folklore of East Anglia. However, the book vanished into obscurity soon after publication, and has never been reprinted until now. Featuring witchcraft, ghosts, charms, traditional cures, legendary tales and an assortment of terrifying spectres (including East Anglia's demon dog, Black Shuck), Margaret James's book is an important source for the folklore current in the Waveney Valley and Suffolk coast in the late 19th century. This critical edition, with an introduction and detailed notes by the folklorist Francis Young, makes available for the first time a rare and elusive book on the supernatural folklore of Norfolk and Suffolk.

ISBN 9780992640460
126pp.
Available from lulu.com

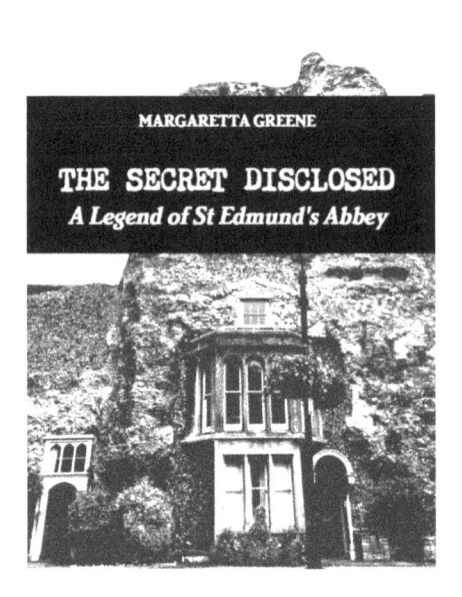

Margaretta Greene, *The Secret Disclosed: A Legend of St Edmund's Abbey*

In 1860, 23 year-old Margaretta Greene was inspired by unexplained phenomena in her family home (which was built into the ruins of the Abbey of Bury St Edmunds) to write a historical novella which gave a narrative to Bury St Edmunds' best-known ghost, the infamous 'Grey Lady' who haunts the ruins of St Edmunds Abbey. Greene told the story of Maude Carew, a nun whose desperate love for a monk of St Edmunds Abbey leads her to conspire with Queen Margaret of Anjou and murder King Henry VI's uncle, Humphrey Duke of Gloucester. The novella proved so sensational in Victorian Bury that it even provoked a riot, but until now it has never been republished and has remained a scarce and elusive work. This edition reprints the original text of Greene's novella along with an extensive introduction by historian Francis Young. Fully referenced with an index and bibliography, this is an authoritative study of Greene's novella as well as an edition of the text.

ISBN 9780992640477
88pp., black and white illustrations
Available from lulu.com

Lightning Source UK Ltd.
Milton Keynes UK
UKHW051534130123
415223UK00019B/1519

9 781470 960209